Praise for
THE ANNIVERSARY DAY SAGA

"Set in the not too distant future, the latest entry in Rusch's popular sf thriller series combines fast-paced action, beautifully conflicted protagonists, and a distinctly 'sf noir' feel to tell a complex and far-reaching mystery."

—*Library Journal* on *Anniversary Day*

"The Retrieval Artist universe is rich and exciting, and Rusch's characters are real beings (Human and otherwise) struggling against overwhelming odds. The thrills are nonstop, and the tension keeps increasing with each successive book [in the Anniversary Day Saga]. If you're a nail-biter, you might want to wear gloves for these."

—*Analog*

"[The Anniversary Day Saga is] one of the top science fiction sagas in recent years."

—*The Midwest Book Review*

"… the Anniversary Day Saga could become a milestone in the field."

—*Amazing Stories*

THE RETRIEVAL ARTIST SERIES:

The Anniversary Day Saga:

Other Stories:

INHUMAN GARBAGE

A RETRIEVAL ARTIST UNIVERSE NOVELLA

KRISTINE KATHRYN RUSCH

*wmg*PUBLISHING

Inhuman Garbage

Published 2016 by WMG Publishing
www.wmgpublishing.com
First published in *Asimov's Science Fiction*, March 2015
Cover art copyright © Rolffimages/Dreamstime
Book and cover design copyright © 2016 by WMG Publishing
Cover design by Allyson Longueira/WMG Publishing
ISBN-13: 978-1-56146-769-3
ISBN-10: 1-56146-769-3

INHUMAN GARBAGE

A RETRIEVAL ARTIST UNIVERSE NOVELLA

1

DETECTIVE NOELLE DERICCI opened the top of the waste crate. The smell of rotting produce nearly hid the faint smell of urine and feces. A woman's body curled on top of the compost pile as if she had fallen asleep.

She hadn't, though. Her eyes were open.

DeRicci couldn't see any obvious cause of death. The woman's skin might have been copper colored when she was alive, but death had turned it sallow. Her hair was pulled back into a tight bun, undisturbed by whatever killed her. She wore a gray and tan pantsuit that seemed more practical than flattering.

DeRicci put the lid down, and resisted the urge to remove her thin gloves. They itched. They always itched. Because she used department gloves rather than buying her own, and they never fit properly.

She rubbed her fingers together, as if something from the crate could have gotten through the gloves, and turned around. Nearly one hundred identical containers lined up behind it. More arrived hourly from all over Armstrong, the largest city on Earth's Moon.

The entire interior of the warehouse smelled faintly of organic material gone bad. She was only in one section of the warehouse. There were dozens of others, and at the end of each, was a conveyer belt that took the waste crate, mulched it, and then sent the material for use in the Growing Pits outside Armstrong's dome.

The crates were cleaned in a completely different section of the warehouse, and then sent back into the city for reuse.

Not every business recycled its organic produce for the Growing Pits, but almost all of the restaurants and half of the grocery stores did. DeRicci's apartment building sent organic food waste into bins that came here as well.

The owner of the warehouse, Najib Ansel, stood next to the nearest row of crates. He wore a blue smock over matching blue trousers, and blue booties on his feet. Blue gloves stuck out of his pocket, and a blue mask hung around his neck.

"How did you find her?" DeRicci asked.

Ansel nodded at the ray of blue light that hovered above the crate, then toed the floor.

"The weight was off," he said. "The crate was too heavy."

DeRicci looked down.

"I take it you have sensors in the floor?" she asked.

"Along the orange line."

She didn't see an orange line. She moved slightly, then saw it. It really wasn't a line, more a series of orange rectangles, long enough to hold the crates, and too short to measure anything beside them.

"So you lifted the lid…" DeRicci started.

"No, sir," Ansel said, using the traditional honorific for someone with more authority.

DeRicci wasn't sure why she had more authority than he did. She had looked him up on her way here. He owned a multimillion dollar industry, which made its fortune charging for waste removal from the city itself, and then reselling that waste at a low price to the Growing Pits.

She had known this business existed, but she hadn't paid a lot of attention to it until an hour ago. She had felt a shock of recognition when she saw the name of the business in the download that sent her here: Ansel Management was scrawled on the side of every waste container in every recycling room in the city.

Najib Ansel had a near monopoly in Armstrong, and had warehouses in six other domed communities. According to her admittedly cursory research, he had filed for permits to work in two new communities just this week.

So the fact that he was in standard worker gear, just like his employees, amazed her. She would have thought a mogul like Ansel would be in a gigantic office somewhere making deals, rather than standing on the floor of the main warehouse just outside Armstrong's dome.

Even though he used the honorific, he didn't say anything more. Clearly, Ansel was going to make her work for information.

"Okay," DeRicci said. "The crate was too heavy. Then what?"

"Then we activated the sensors, to see what was inside the crate." He looked up at the blue light again. Obviously that was the sensor.

"Show me how that works," she said.

He rubbed his fingers together—probably activating some kind of chip. The light came down and broadened, enveloping the crate. Information flowed above it, mostly in chemical compounds and other numbers. She was amazed she recognized that the symbols were compounds. She wondered where she had picked that up.

"No visuals?" she asked.

"Not right away." He reached up to the holographic display. The numbers kept scrolling. "You see, there's really nothing out of the ordinary here. Even her clothes must be made of some kind of organic material. So my people couldn't figure out what was causing the extra weight."

"You didn't find this, then?" she asked.

"No, sir," he said.

"I'd like to talk with the person who did," she said.

"She's over there." He nodded toward a small room off to the side of the crates.

DeRicci suppressed a sigh. Of course he cleared the employee off the floor. Anything to make a cop's job harder.

4

"All right," DeRicci said, not trying to hide her annoyance. "How did your 'people' discover the extra weight?"

"When the numbers didn't show anything," he said, "they had the system scan for a large piece. Sometimes, when crates come in from the dome, someone dumps something directly into the crate without paying attention to weight and size restrictions."

Those were hard to ignore. DeRicci vividly remembered the first time she tried to dump something of the wrong size into a recycling crate. She dumped a rotted roast she had never managed to cook (back in the days when she actually believed she could cook). She'd put it into the crate behind her then-apartment building. The damn crate beeped at her, and when she didn't remove the roast fast enough for the stupid thing, it actually started to yell at her, telling her that she wasn't following the rules.

There was a way to turn off the alarms, but she and her building superintendent didn't know it. Clearly, someone else did.

"So," DeRicci said, "the system scanned, and…?"

"Registered something larger," he said somewhat primly. "That's when my people switched the information feed to visual, and got the surprise of their lives."

She would wager. She wondered if they thought the woman was sleeping. She wasn't going to ask him that question; she'd save it for the person who actually found the body.

"When did they call you?" she asked.

"After they visually confirmed the body," he said.

"Meaning what?" she asked. "They saw it on the feed or they actually lifted the lid?"

"On the feed," he said.

"Where was this?" she asked.

He pointed to a small booth that hovered over the floor. The booth clearly operated on the same tech that the flying cars in Armstrong used. The booth was smaller than the average car, however, and was clear on all four sides. Only the bottom appeared to have some kind of structure, probably to hide all the mechanics.

"Is someone in the booth?" she asked.

"We always have someone monitoring the floor," he said, "but I put someone new up there, so that the team which discovered the body can talk to you."

DeRicci supposed he had put the entire team in one room, together, so that they could align their stories. But she didn't say anything like that. No sense antagonizing Ansel. He was helping her.

"We're going to need to shut down this part of your line," she said. "Everything in this part of the warehouse will need to be examined."

To her surprise, he didn't protest. Of course, if he had protested, she would have had him shut down the entire warehouse.

Maybe he had dealt with the police before.

"So," she said, "who actually opened the lid on this container?"

"I did," he said quietly.

6

She hadn't expected that. "Tell me about it."

"The staff contacted me after they saw the body."

"On your links?" she asked. Everyone had internal links for communication, and the links could be set up with varying degrees of privacy. She would wager that the entire communication system inside Ansel Management was on its own dedicated link.

"Yes," he said. "The staff contacted me on my company link."

"I'd like to have copies of that contact," she said.

"Sure." He wasn't acting like someone who had anything to hide. In fact, he was acting like someone who had been through this before.

"What did your staff tell you?" she asked.

His lips turned upward. Someone might have called that expression a smile, but it wasn't. It was rueful.

"They told me that there was a woman in crate A1865."

DeRicci made a mental note about the number. Before this investigation was over, she'd learn everything about this operation, from the crate numbering system to the way that the conveyer operated to the actual mulching process.

"That's what they said?" she asked. "A woman in the crate?"

"Crate A1865," he repeated, as if he wanted that detail to be exactly right.

"What did you think when you heard that?" DeRicci asked.

He shook his head, then sighed. "I—we've had this happen before, Detective. Not for more than a year,

7

but we've found bodies. Usually homeless people in the crates near the Port, people who came into Armstrong and can't get out. Sometimes we get an alien or two sleeping in the crates. The Oranjanie view rotting produce as a luxury, and they look human from some angles."

The Port of Armstrong was the main spaceport onto the Moon, and also functioned as the gateway to Earth. Member species of the Earth Alliance had to stop in Armstrong first, before traveling to Earth. Some travelers never made it into Earth's protected zone, and got stuck on the Moon itself.

Right now, however, she had no reason to suspect alien involvement in this crime. She preferred working human-on-human crime. It made the investigation so much easier.

"You've found human bodies in your crates before," she clarified.

"Yeah," he said.

"And the police have investigated?"

"All of the bodies, alien and human," he said. "Different precincts, usually, and different time periods. My grandmother started this business over 100 years ago. She found bodies even way back then."

DeRicci guessed it would make sense to hide a body in one of the crates. Or someone would think it made sense.

"Do you think that bodies have gotten through the mulching process?" It took her a lot of strength not to look at the conveyer belt as she asked that question.

"I don't think a lot got through," he said. "I know some did. Back in my grandmother's day. She's the one who set up the safeguards. We might have had a few glitches after the safeguards were in place, before we knew how well they worked, but I can guarantee nothing has gone through since I started managing this company twenty-five years ago."

DeRicci tried not to shudder as she thought about human flesh serving as compost at the Growing Pits. She hated Moon-grown food, and she had a hunch she was going to hate it more after this case.

But she had to keep asking questions.

"You said you can guarantee it," she repeated.

He nodded.

"What if someone cut up the body?" she asked.

He grimaced. "The pieces would have to be small to get past our weight and size restrictions. Forgive me for being graphic, but no full arms or legs or torsos or heads. Maybe fingers and toes. We have nanoprobes on these things, looking for human DNA. But the probes are coating the lining of the crates. If someone buried a finger in the middle of some rotting lettuce, we might miss it."

She turned so that he wouldn't see her reaction. She forced herself to swallow some bile back, and wished she had some savings. She wanted to go home and purge her refrigerator of anything grown on the Moon, and buy expensive Earth-grown produce.

But she couldn't afford that, not on a detective's salary.

"Fair enough," she said, surprised she could sound so calm when she was so thoroughly grossed out. "No full bodies have gone through in at least twenty-five years. But you've seen quite a few. How many?"

"I don't know," he said. "I'd have to check the records."

That surprised her. It meant there were enough that he couldn't keep track. "Any place where they show up the most often?"

"The Port," he said. "There's a lot of homeless in that neighborhood."

Technically, they weren't homeless. They were people who lived on the city's charity. A lot of small cubicle sized rooms existed on the Port blocks, and anyone who couldn't afford their own home or ended up stranded and unemployable in the city could stay in one of the cubicles for six months, no questions asked.

After six months, they needed to move to long-term city services, which were housed elsewhere. She wanted to ask if anyone had turned up in those neighborhoods, but she'd do that after she looked at his records.

"I'm confused," she said. "Do these people crawl into the crates and die?"

The crate didn't look like it was sealed so tightly that the person couldn't get oxygen.

"Some of them," he said. "They're usually high or drunk."

"And the rest?" she asked.

"Obviously someone has put them there," he said.

"A different someone each time, I assume," she said.

He shrugged. "I let the police investigate. I don't ask questions."

"You don't ask questions about dead people in your crates?"

His face flushed. She had finally gotten to him.

"Believe it or not, Detective," he snapped, "I don't like to think about it. I'm very proud of this business. We provide a service that enables the cities on the Moon to not only have food, but to have *great* food. Sometimes our system gets fouled up by crazy people, and I *hate* that. We've gone to great lengths to prevent it. That's why you're here. Because our systems *work*."

"I didn't mean to offend you," she lied. "This is all new to me, so I'm going to ask some very ignorant questions at times."

He looked annoyed, but he nodded.

"What part of town did this crate come from?" she asked.

"The Port," he said tiredly.

She should have expected that, after he had mentioned the Port a few times.

"Was the body in the crate when it was picked up at the Port?" she asked.

"The weight was the same from Port to here," he said. "Weight gets recorded at pickup but flagged near the conveyer. The entire system is automated until the crates get to the warehouse. Besides, we don't have the ability to investigate anything inside Armstrong. There are a lot of regulations on things that are considered garbage inside the dome. If we violate those, we'll get black marks against our license, and if we get too many black marks in a year, we could lose that license."

More stuff she didn't know. City stuff, regulatory stuff. The kinds of things she always ignored.

And things she would probably have to investigate now.

"Do you know her?" DeRicci asked, hoping to catch him off balance.

"Her?" He looked confused for a moment. Then he looked at the crate, and his flush grew deeper. "You mean, *her*?"

"Yes," DeRicci said. Just from his reaction she knew his response. He didn't know the woman. And the idea that she was inside one of his crates upset him more than he wanted to say.

Which was probably why he was the person talking to DeRicci now.

"No," he said. "I don't know her, and I don't recognize her. We didn't run any recognition programs on her either. We figured you all would do that."

"No one touched her? No one checked her for identification chips?"

"I'm the one who opened the crate," he said. "I saw her, I saw that her eyes were open, and then I closed the lid. I leave the identifying to you all."

"Do you know all your employees, Mr. Ansel?"

"By name," he said.

"By look," she said.

He shook his head. "I have nearly three hundred employees in Armstrong alone."

"But you just said you know their names. You know all three hundred employees by name?"

He smiled absently, which seemed like a rote response. He'd responded to this kind of thing before.

"I have an eidetic memory," he said. "If I've seen a name, then I remember it."

"An eidetic memory for names, but not faces? I've never heard of that," DeRicci said.

"I haven't met all of my employees," he said. "But I go over the pay amounts every week before they get sent to the employees' accounts. I see the names. I rarely see the faces."

"So you wouldn't know if she worked here," DeRicci said.

"Here?" he asked. "Here I would know. I come here every day. If she worked in one of the other warehouses or in transport or in sales, I wouldn't know that."

"Did this crate go somewhere else before coming to this warehouse?" DeRicci asked.

"No," Ansel said. "Each crate is assigned a number. That number puts it in a location, and then when the crate fills, it gets swapped out with another. The crate comes to the same warehouse each time, without deviation. And since that system is automated, as I mentioned, I know that it doesn't go awry."

"Can someone stop the crate in transit and add a body?"

"No," he said. "I can show you if you want."

She shook her head. That would be a good job for her partner, Rayvon Lake. Rayvon still hadn't arrived, the bastard. DeRicci would have to report him pretty soon. He had gotten very lax about crime scenes, leaving them to her. He left most everything to her, and she hated it.

He was a lazy detective—twenty years in the position—and he saw her as an upstart who needed to be put in her place.

She wouldn't have minded if he did his job. Well, that wasn't exactly true. She would have minded. She hated people who disliked her. But she wouldn't be considering filing a report on him if he actually did the work he was supposed to do.

She would get Lake to handle the transport information by telling him she wasn't smart enough to understand it. It would mean that she'd have to suffer through an explanation later in the case, but maybe by then, she'd either have this thing solved or she'd have a new partner.

A woman could hope, after all.

"One of the other detectives will look into the transport process," DeRicci said. "I'm just trying to cover the basics here, so we start looking in the right place. Can outsiders come into this warehouse?"

"And get into one of our crates?" Ansel asked. "No. Look."

He touched the edge of the lid, and she heard a loud snap.

"It's sealed shut now," he said.

She didn't like the sound of that snap.

"If I were in there," she asked, "could I breathe through that seal?"

"Yes," he said. "For about two days, if need be. But it doesn't seal shut like that until it leaves the transport and crosses the threshold here at the warehouse. So there's no way anyone could crawl in here at the warehouse."

"All right," DeRicci said. "So, let me be sure I understand you. The only place that someone could either place a body into a crate or crawl into it on their own is on site."

"Yes," Ansel said. "We try to encourage composting, so we allow bypassers to stuff something into a crate. We search for non-organic material at the site, and flag the crates with non-organic material so they can be cleaned."

"Clothing is organic?" DeRicci asked.

"Much of it, yes," Ansel said. "Synthetics aren't good hosts for nanoproducts, so most people wear clothing made from recycled organic material."

DeRicci's skin literally crawled. She hadn't known that. She wasn't an organic kind of woman. She preferred fake stuff, much to the dismay of her friends.

"All right," she said. "I'm going to talk with your people in a minute. I'll want to know what they know. And I'll need to see your records on previous incidents."

She didn't check to see if he had sent her anything on her links. She didn't want downloads to confuse her sense of the crime scene. She liked to make her own opinions, and she did that by being thorough.

Detectives like Rayvon Lake gathered as much information as possible, multitasking as they walked through a crime scene. She believed they missed most of the important details while doing that, and that led to a lot of side roads and wasted time.

And, if she could prove it (if she had time to prove it), a lot of false convictions. She had caught Lake twice trying to close a case by accusing an innocent person who was convenient, rather than doing the hard leg work required of a good investigator.

Ansel fluttered near her for a moment. She inclined her head toward the room where the staff had gathered, knowing she was inviting him to contaminate her witnesses even more, but she had a hunch none of them were going to be useful to the investigation anyway.

"Before you go," she said, just in case he didn't take the hint, "could you unseal this crate for me?"

"Oh, yes, sorry," he said, and ran his fingers along the side again. It snapped one more time, then popped up slightly.

DeRicci thanked him, and pulled back the lid. The crate was deep—up to DeRicci's ribs—and filled with unidentifiable bits of rotting food. The woman lay on top of them, hands cradled under her cheek, feet tucked together.

DeRicci couldn't imagine anyone just curling up here, even at the bidding of someone else. But people did strange things for strange reasons, and she wasn't going to rule it out.

She put the lid down and then looked at the warehouse again. She would need the numbers, but she suspected thousands of crates went through Ansel's facilities around the Moon daily.

Done properly, it would be a perfect way to dispose of bodies and all kinds of other things that no one wanted to see. She wondered how many others knew about this facility and how it worked.

She suspected she would have to find out.

2

GETTING THE CRIME scene unit to a warehouse outside of the dome took more work than Ethan Broduer liked to do. Fortunately, he was a deputy coroner, which meant he couldn't control the crime scene unit. Someone with more seniority had to handle requisitioning the right vehicle from the Police Department yards outside the dome, and making certain the team had the right equipment.

Broduer came to the warehouse via train. The ride was only five minutes long, but it made him nervous.

He was born inside the dome, and he hated leaving it for any reason at all, especially for a reason involving work. So much of his work had to do with temperature and conditions, and if the body had been in an airless environment at all, it had an impact on every aspect of his job.

He was relieved when he arrived at the warehouse and learned that the body had never gone outside of an Earth Normal environment. However, he was annoyed to see that he would be working with Noelle DeRicci.

She was notoriously difficult and demanding, and often asked coroners to redo something or double-check their findings. She'd caught him in several mistakes, which he found embarrassing.

Then she had had the gall to tell him that he should probably double-check all of his work, considering its shoddy quality.

She stood next to a crate, the only one of thousands that was open. She was rumpled—she was always rumpled—and her curly black hair looked messier than usual.

When she saw him approach, she glared at him.

"Oh, lucky me," she said.

Broduer bit back a response. He'd been recording everything since he got off the train inside the warehouse's private platform, and he didn't want to show any animosity toward DeRicci on anything that might go to court.

"Just show me the body and I'll get to work," he said.

She raised her eyebrows at the word "work," and she didn't have to add anything to convey her meaning. She didn't think Broduer worked at all.

"My biggest priority at the moment is an identification," DeRicci said.

And his biggest priority was to do this investigation right. But he didn't say that. Instead he looked at the dozens of crates spread out before him.

"Which one am I dealing with?" he asked, pleased that he could sound so calm in the face of her rudeness.

She placed a hand on the crate behind her. He was pleased to see that she wore gloves. He had worked with her partner Rayvon Lake before, and Lake had to be reminded to follow any kind of procedure.

But Broduer didn't see Lake anywhere.

"Have you had cases involving the waste crates before?" DeRicci asked Broduer.

"No," he said, not adding that he tried to pass anything outside the dome onto anyone else, "but I've heard about cases involving them. I guess it's not that uncommon."

"Hmm," she said looking toward a room at the far end of the large warehouse. "And here I thought they were."

Broduer was going to argue his point when he realized that DeRicci wasn't talking to him now. She was arguing with someone she had already spoken to.

"Can you get me information on that?" DeRicci asked Broduer.

He hated it when detectives wanted him to do their work for them. "It's in the records."

DeRicci made a low, growly sound, like he had irritated her beyond measure.

So he decided to tweak her a bit more. "Just search for warehouses and recycling and crates—"

"I know," she said. "I was hoping your office already had statistics."

"I'm sure we do, Detective," he said, moving past her, "but you want me to figure out what killed this poor creature, right? Not dig into old cases."

"I think the old cases might be relevant," she said.

He shrugged. He didn't care what was or wasn't relevant to her investigation. His priority was dealing with this body.

"Excuse me," he said, and slipped on his favorite pair of gloves. Then he raised the lid on the crate.

The woman inside was maybe thirty. She had been pretty too, before her eyes had filmed over and her cheeks sunk in.

She had clearly died in an Earth Normal environment, and she hadn't left that environment, as advertised. He would have to do some research to figure out if the presence of rotting food had an impact on the body's decomposition, but that was something to worry about later.

Then Broduer glanced up. "I'll have information for you in a while," he said to DeRicci.

"Just give me a name," she said. "We haven't traced anything."

He didn't want to move the body yet. He didn't even want to touch it, because he was afraid of disturbing some important evidence.

The corpse's hands were tucked under her head, so he couldn't just run the identification chips everyone had buried in their palms.

So he used the coroner's office facial recognition program. It had a record of every single human who lived in

Armstrong, and was constantly updated with information from the arrivals and departures sections of the city every single day.

"Initial results show that her name is Sonja Mycenae. She was born here, and moved off-Moon with her family ten years ago. She returned one month ago to work as a nanny for...."

He paused, stunned at the name that turned up.

"For?" DeRicci pushed.

Broduer looked up. He could feel the color draining from his face.

"Luc Deshin," he said quietly. "She works for Luc Deshin."

3

Luc Deshin.

DeRicci hadn't expected that name.

Luc Deshin ran a corporation called Deshin Enterprises that the police department flagged and monitored continually. Everyone in Armstrong knew that Deshin controlled a huge crime syndicate that trafficked in all sorts of illegal and banned substances. The bulk of Deshin's business had moved off-Moon, but he had gotten his start as an average street thug, rising, as those kids often do, through murder and targeted assassination into a position of power, using the deaths of others to advance his own career.

"Luc Deshin needed a nanny?" DeRicci sounded confused.

"He married a few years ago," Broduer said, as he bent over the body again. "I guess they had kids."

"And didn't like the nanny." DeRicci whistled. "Talk about a high stress job."

She glanced at that room filled with the employees who found the body. There was a lot of work to be done here, but none of it was as important as catching Deshin by surprise with this investigation.

If he killed this Sonja Mycenae, then he would be expecting the police's appearance. But he might not expect them so soon.

Or maybe he had always used the waste crates to dump his bodies. No one had ever been able to pin a murder on him.

Perhaps this was why.

She needed to leave. But before she did, she sent a message to Lake. Only she sent it using the standard police links, not the encoded link any other officer would use with her partner. She wanted it on record that Lake hadn't shown up yet.

Rayvon, you need to get here ASAP. There are employees to interview. I'm following a lead, but someone has to supervise the crime scene unit. Someone sent Deputy Coroner Broduer and he doesn't have supervisory authority.

She didn't wait for Lake's response. Before he said anything, she sent another message to her immediate supervisor, Chief of Detectives Andrea Gumiela, this time through an encoded private link.

This case has ties to Deshin Enterprises, DeRicci sent. *I'm going there now, but we need a* good *team on this. It's not some random death. It needs to be done perfectly. Between Broduer and Lake, we're off to a bad start.*

She didn't wait for Gumiela to respond either. In fact, after sending that message, DeRicci shut off all but her emergency links.

She didn't want Gumiela to tell her to stay on site, and she didn't want to hear Lake's invective when he realized she had essentially chastised him in front of the entire department.

"Make sure no one leaves," DeRicci said to Broduer.

He looked up, panicked. "I don't have the authority."

"Pretend," she snapped, and walked away from him.

She needed to get to Luc Deshin, and she needed to get to him now.

4

LUC DESHIN GRABBED his long-waisted overcoat and headed down the stairs. So a police detective wanted to meet with him. He wished he found such things unusual. But they weren't.

The police liked to harass him. Less now than in the past. They'd had a frustrating time pinning anything on him.

He always found it ironic that the crimes they accused him of were crimes he'd never think of committing, and the crimes he had committed—long ago and far away—were crimes they had never heard of.

Now, all of his activities were legal. Just-inside-the-law legal, but legal nonetheless.

Or so his cadre of lawyers kept telling the local courts, and the local judges—at least the ones he would find himself in front of—always believed his lawyers.

So, a meeting like this, coming in the middle of the day, was an annoyance, and nothing more.

He used his trip down the stairs to stay in shape. His office was a penthouse on the top floor of the building he'd built to house Deshin Enterprises years ago. He used to love that office, but he liked it less since he and his wife Gerda brought a baby into their lives.

He smiled at the thought of Paavo. They had adopted him—sort of. They had drawn up some legal papers and wills that the lawyers assured him would stand any challenge should he and Gerda die suddenly.

But Deshin and Gerda had decided against an actual adoption given Deshin's business practices and his reputation in Armstrong. They were worried that some judge would deem them unfit, based on Deshin's reputation.

Plus, Paavo was the child of two Disappeareds, making the adoption situation even more difficult. The Earth Alliance's insistence that local laws prevailed when crimes were committed meant that humans were often subjected to alien laws, laws that made no sense at all. Many humans didn't like being forced to lose a limb as punishment for chopping down an exotic tree, or giving up a child because they'd broken food laws on a different planet.

Those who could afford to get new names and new identities did so rather than accept their punishment under Earth Alliance law. Those people Disappeared.

Paavo's parents had Disappeared within weeks of his birth, leaving him to face whatever legal threat those aliens could dream up.

Paavo, alone, at four months.

Fortunately, Deshin and Gerda had sources inside Armstrong's family services, which they had done for just this sort of reason. Both Deshin and Gerda had had difficult childhoods—to say the least. They knew what it was like to be unwanted.

Their initial plan had been to bring several unwanted children into their homes, but after they met Paavo, a brilliant baby with his own special needs, they decided to put that plan on hold. If they could only save Paavo, that would be enough.

But they were just a month into life with the baby, and they knew that any more children would take a focus that, at the moment at least, Paavo's needs wouldn't allow.

Deshin reached the bottom of the stairwell, ran a hand through his hair, and then walked through the double doors. His staff kept the detective in the lobby.

She was immediately obvious, even though she wasn't in uniform. A slightly disheveled woman with curly black hair and a sharp, intelligent face, she wasn't looking around like she was supposed to be.

Most new visitors to Deshin Enterprises either pretended to be unimpressed with the real marble floors, the imported wood paneling, and the artwork that constantly shifted on the walls and ceiling. Or the visitors gaped openly at all of it.

This detective did neither. Instead, she scanned the people in the lobby—all staff, all there to guard him and keep an eye on her.

She would be difficult. He could tell that just from her body language. He wasn't used to dealing with someone from the Armstrong Police Department who was intelligent *and* difficult to impress.

He walked toward her, and as he reached her, he extended his hand.

"Detective," he said warmly. "I'm Luc Deshin."

She wiped her hands on her stained shirt, and just as he thought she was going to take his hand in greeting, she shoved her hands into the pockets of her ill-fitting black pants.

"I know who you are," she said.

She deliberately failed to introduce herself, probably as a power play. He could play back, ask to see the badge chip embedded in the palm of her hand, but he didn't feel like playing.

She had already wasted enough of his time.

So he took her name, Noelle DeRicci, from the building's security records, and declined to look at her service record. He had it if he needed it.

"What can I do for you then, Detective?" He was going to charm her, even if that took a bit of strength to ignore the games.

"I'd like to speak somewhere private," she said.

He smiled. "No one is near us, and we have no recording devices in this part of the lobby. If you like, we can go outside. There's a lovely coffee shop across the street."

Her eyes narrowed. He watched her think: did she ask to go to his office and get denied, or did she just play along?

"The privacy is for you," she said, "but okay...."

She sounded dubious, a nice little trick. A less secure man would then invite her into the office.

Deshin waited. He learned that middle managers—and that was what detectives truly were—always felt the press of time. He never had enough time for anything and yet, as the head of his own corporation, he also had all the time in the universe.

"I'm here about Sonja Mycenae," she said.

Sonja. The nanny he had fired just that morning. Well, fired wasn't an accurate term. He had deliberately avoided firing her. He had eliminated her position.

He and Gerda had decided that Sonja wasn't affectionate enough toward their son. In fact, she had seemed a bit cold toward him. And once Deshin and Gerda started that conversation about Sonja's attitudes, they realized they didn't like having someone visit their home every day, and they didn't like giving up any time with Paavo.

Both Gerda and Deshin had worried, given their backgrounds, that they wouldn't know how to nurture a baby, but Sonja had taught them that training mattered a lot less than actual love.

"I understand she works for you," the detective said.

"She work*ed* for me," he said.

Something changed in the detective's face. Something small. He felt uneasy for the first time.

"Tell me what this is about, Detective," he said.

"It's about Sonja Mycenae," she repeated.

"Yes, you said that. What exactly has she done?" he asked.

"Why don't you tell me why she no longer works for you," the detective said.

"My wife and I decided that we didn't need a nanny for our son. I called Sonja to the office this morning, and let her know that, effective immediately, her employment was terminated through no fault of her own."

"Do you have footage of that conversation?" the detective asked.

"I do, and it's protected. You'll need permission from both of us or a warrant before I can give it to you."

The detective raised her eyebrows. "I'm sure you can forgo the formalities, Mr. Deshin."

"I'm sure that many people do, Detective," he said, "however, it's my understanding that an employee's records are confidential. You may get a warrant if you like. Otherwise, I'm going to protect Sonja's privacy."

"Why would you do that, Mr. Deshin?"

"Believe it or not, I follow the rules." He managed to say that without sarcasm.

The detective grunted as if she didn't believe him. "What made you decide to terminate her position today?"

"I told you," Deshin said, keeping his voice bland even though he was getting annoyed. "My wife and I decided we didn't need a nanny to help us raise our son."

"You might want to share that footage with me without wasting time on a warrant, Mr. Deshin," the detective said.

"Why would I do that, Detective? I'm not even sure why you're asking about Sonja. What has she done?"

"She has died, Mr. Deshin."

The words hung between them. He frowned. The detective had finally caught him off guard.

For the first time, he did not know how to respond. He probably needed one of his lawyers here. Any time his name came up in an investigation, he was automatically the first suspect.

But in this case, he had nothing to do with Sonja's death. So he would act accordingly, and let the lawyers handle the mess.

"What happened?" he asked softly.

He had known Sonja since she was a child. She was the daughter of a friend. That was one of the many reasons he had hired her, because he had known her.

Even then, she hadn't turned out as expected. He remembered an affectionate happy girl. The nanny who had come to his house didn't seem to know how to smile at all. There had been no affection in her.

And when he last saw her, she'd been crying and pleading with him to keep her job. He actually had to have security drag her out of his office.

"We don't know what happened," the detective said.

That sentence could mean a lot. It could mean that they didn't know what happened at all or that they didn't know if her death was by natural causes or by murder. It could also mean that they didn't know exactly what or who caused the death, but that they suspected murder.

Since he was facing a detective and not a beat officer, he knew they suspected murder.

"Where did it happen?" Deshin asked.

"We don't know that either," the detective said.

He snapped, "Then how do you know she's dead?"

Again, that slight change in the detective's face. Apparently he had finally hit on the correct question.

"Because workers found her in a waste crate in a warehouse outside the dome."

"Outside the dome…?" That didn't make sense to him. Sonja hadn't even owned an environmental suit. She had hated them with a passion. "She died outside the dome?"

"I didn't say that, Mr. Deshin," the detective said.

He let out a breath. "Look, Detective, I'm cooperating here, but you need to work with me. I saw Sonja this morning, eliminated her position, and watched her leave my office. Then I went to work. I haven't gone out of the building all day."

"But your people have," the detective said.

He felt a thin thread of fury, and he suppressed it. Everyone assumed that his people murdered other people according to some whim. That simply was not true.

"Detective," he said calmly. "If I wanted Sonja dead, why would I terminate her employment this morning?"

"I have only your word for that," the detective said. "Unless you give me the footage."

"And I have only your word that she's dead," he said.

The detective pressed her hands together, then separated them. A hologram appeared between them—

a young woman, looking as if she had fallen asleep in a meadow. Until he looked closely, and saw that the "meadow" was bits of food, and the young woman's eyes were open and filmy.

It was Sonja.

"My God," he said.

"If you give me the footage," the detective said, "and it confirms what you say, then you'll be in the clear. If you wait, then we're going to assume it was doctored."

Deshin glared at her. She was good—and she was right. The longer he waited, the less credibility he would have.

"I'm going to consult with my attorneys," he said. "If they believe that this information has use to you and it doesn't cause me any legal liabilities, then you will receive it from them within the hour."

The detective crossed her arms. "I suggest that you send it to me now. I will promise you that I will not look at anything until you or your attorneys say that I can."

It was an odd compromise, but one that *would* protect him. If she believed he would doctor the footage, then having the footage in her possession wouldn't harm him.

But he didn't know the laws on something this arcane.

"How's this, detective," he said. "My staff will give you a chip with the information on it. You may not put the chip into any device or watch it until I've consulted with my attorneys. You will wait here while I do so."

"Seems fine to me," the detective said. "I've got all the time in the world."

5

SHE DIDN'T HAVE all the time in the world, of course. DeRicci was probably getting all kinds of messages on her links from Lake and Gumiela and Broduer and everyone else, telling her she was stupid or needed or something.

She didn't care. She certainly wasn't going to turn her links back on. She was close to something.

She had actually surprised the Great Luc Deshin, Criminal Mastermind.

He pivoted, and moved three steps away from her. He was clearly contacting someone on his links, but using private encoded links.

A staff member approached, a woman DeRicci hadn't seen before. The woman, dressed in a black suit, extended a hand covered with gold rings.

"If you'll come this way, Detective DeRicci..."

DeRicci shook her head. "Mr. Deshin promised me a chip. I'm staying here until I get it."

The woman opened her other hand. In it was a chip case the size of a thumbnail. The case was clear, and inside, DeRicci saw another case—blue, with a filament thinner than an eyelash.

"Here is your chip, Detective," the woman said. "I've been instructed to take you—"

"I don't care," DeRicci said. "I'll take the chip, and I'll wait right here. You have my word that I won't open either case, and I won't watch anything until I get the okay."

The woman's eyes glazed slightly. Clearly, she was seeing if that was all right.

Then she focused on DeRicci, and bowed her head slightly.

"As you wish, Detective."

She handed DeRicci the case. It was heavier than it looked. It probably had a lot of protections built in, so that she couldn't activate anything through the case.

Not that she had the technical ability to do any of that, even if she wanted to.

She sighed. She had a fluttery feeling that she had just been outmaneuvered.

Then she made herself watch Deshin. He seemed truly distressed at the news of Sonja Mycenae's death. If DeRicci had to put money on it, she would say that he hadn't known she was dead and he hadn't ordered the death.

But he was also well known for his business acumen, his criminal savvy, and his ability to beat a clear case against him. A man didn't get a reputation like that by being easy to read.

She closed her fist around the chip case, clasped her hands behind her back, and waited, watching Luc Deshin the entire time.

6

DESHIN HADN'T GONE FAR. He wanted to keep an eye on the detective. He'd learned in the past that police officers had a tendency to wander, and observe things they shouldn't.

He had staff in various parts of the lobby to prevent the detective from doing just that.

Through private, encoded links, he had contacted his favorite attorney, Martin Oberholtz. For eight years, Oberholtz had managed the most delicate cases for Deshin—always knowing how far the law could bend before it broke.

Before I tell you what to do, Oberholtz was saying on their link, *I want to see the footage.*

It'll take time, Deshin sent.

Ach, Oberholtz sent. *I'll just bill you for it. Send it to me.*

I already have, Deshin sent.

I'll be in contact shortly, Oberholtz sent, and signed off.

Deshin walked to the other side of the lobby. He didn't want to vanish because he didn't want the detective to think he was doing something nefarious.

But he was unsettled. That meeting with Sonja had not gone as he expected.

Over the years, Deshin had probably fired two hundred people personally, and his staff had fired even more. And that didn't count the business relationships he had terminated.

Doing unpleasant things didn't bother him. They usually followed a pattern. But the meeting that morning hadn't followed a pattern that he recognized.

He had spoken quite calmly to Sonja, telling her that he and Gerda had decided to raise Paavo without help. He hadn't criticized Sonja at all. In fact, he had promised her a reference if she wanted it, and he had complimented her on the record, saying that her presence had given him and Gerda the confidence to handle Paavo alone.

He hadn't said that the confidence had come from the fact that Sonja had years of training and she missed the essential ingredient—affection. He had kept everything as neutral and positive as possible, given that he was effectively firing her without firing her.

Midway through his little speech, her eyes widened. He had thought she was going to burst into tears. Instead, she put a shaking hand to her mouth, looking like she had just received news that everything she loved in the world was going to be taken away from her.

He had a moment of confusion—had she actually cared that much about Paavo?—and then he decided it didn't matter; he and Gerda really did want to raise the boy on their own, without any outside help.

"Mr. Deshin," Sonja had said when he finished. "Please, I beg you, do not fire me."

"I'm not firing you, Sonja," he had said. "I just don't have a job for you any longer."

"Please," she said. "I will work here. I will do anything, the lowest of the low. I will do jobs that are disgusting or frightening, anything, Mr. Deshin. Please. Just don't make me leave."

He had never had an employee beg so strenuously to keep her job. It unnerved him. "I don't have any work for you."

"Please, Mr. Deshin." She reached for him and he leaned back. "Please. Don't make me leave."

That was when he sent a message along his links to security. This woman was crazy, and no one on his staff had picked up on it. He felt both relieved and appalled. Relieved that she was going nowhere near Paavo again, and appalled that he had left his beloved little son in her care.

The door opened, and then Sonja screamed "No!" at the top of her lungs. She grabbed at Deshin, and one of his security people pulled her away.

She kicked and fought and screamed and cried all the way through the door. It closed behind her, leaving him alone, but he could still hear her yelling all the way to the elevator.

The incident had unsettled him.

It still unsettled him.

And now, just a few hours later, Sonja was dead.

That couldn't be a coincidence.

It couldn't be a coincidence at all.

7

IT TOOK NEARLY fifteen minutes before Luc Deshin returned. DeRicci had watched him pace on the other side of the lobby, his expression grim.

It was still grim when he reached her.

He nodded at the chip in her hand. "My staff tells me that you have a lot of information on that chip. In addition to the meeting in my office, you'll see Sonja's arrival and her departure. You'll also see that she left through that front door. After she disappeared off our external security cameras, no one on my staff saw her again."

He was being very precise. DeRicci figured his lawyer had told him to do that.

"Thank you," she said, closing her fingers around the case. "I appreciate the cooperation."

"You're welcome," Deshin said, then walked away.

She watched him go. Something about his mood had darkened since she originally spoke to him. Because of the lawyer? Or something else?

It didn't matter. She had the information she needed, at least for the moment.

She would deal with Deshin later if she needed to.

8

DESHIN TOOK THE stairs back to his office. He needed to think, and he didn't want to run into any of his staff on the elevator. Besides, exercise kept his head clear.

He had thought Sonja crazy after her reaction in his office. But what if she knew her life was in danger if she left his employ? Then her behavior made sense.

He wasn't going to say that to the detective, nor had he mentioned it to his lawyer. Deshin was going to investigate this himself.

As he reached the top floor, he sent a message to his head of security, Otto Koos: *My office. Now.*

Deshin went through the doors and stopped, as he always did, looking at the view. He had a 360-degree view of the City of Armstrong. Right now, the dome was set at Dome Daylight, mimicking midday sunlight on Earth. He loved the look of Dome Daylight because it put buildings all over the city in such clear light that it made them look like a beautiful painting or a holographic wall image.

He crossed to his desk, and called up the file on Sonja Mycenae, looking for anything untoward, anything his staff might have missed.

He saw nothing.

She had worked for a family on Earth who had filed monthly reports with the nanny service that had vetted her. The reports were excellent. Sonja had then left the family to come to the Moon, because, apparently, she had been homesick.

He couldn't find anything in a cursory search of that file which showed any contradictory information.

The door to his office opened, and Koos entered. He was a short man with broad shoulders and a way of walking that made him look like he was itching for a fight.

Deshin had known him since they were boys, and trusted Koos with his life. Koos had saved that life more than once.

"Sonja was murdered after she left us this morning," Deshin said.

Koos glanced at the door. "So that was why Armstrong PD was here."

"Yeah," Deshin said, "and it clarifies her reaction. She knew something bad would happen to her."

"She was a plant," Koos said.

"Or something," Deshin said. "We need to know why. Did anyone follow her after she left?"

"You didn't order us to," Koos said, "and I saw no reason to keep track of her. She was crying pretty hard when she walked out, but she never looked back and as far as I could tell, no one was after her."

"The police are going to trace her movements," Deshin said. "We need to as well. But what I want to know is this: What did we miss about this woman? I've already checked her file. I see nothing unusual."

"I'll go over it again," Koos said.

"Don't go over it," Deshin said, feeling a little annoyed. After all, he had just done that, and he didn't need to be double-checked. "Vet her again, as if we were just about to hire her. See what you come up with."

"Yes, sir," Koos said. Normally, he would have left after that, but he didn't. Instead, he held his position.

Deshin suppressed a sigh. Something else was coming his way. "What?"

"When you dismissed her and she reacted badly," Koos said, "I increased security around your wife and child. I'm going to increase it again, and I'm going to make sure you've got extra protection as well."

Deshin opened his mouth, but Koos put up one finger, stopping him.

"Don't argue with me," Koos said. "Something's going on here, and I don't like it."

Deshin smiled. "I wasn't going to argue with you, Otto. I was going to thank you. I hadn't thought to increase security around my family, and it makes sense."

Koos nodded, as if Deshin's praise embarrassed him. Then he left the office.

Deshin watched him go. As soon as he was gone, Deshin contacted Gerda on their private links.

Koos might have increased security, but Deshin wanted to make sure everything was all right.

He used to say that families were a weakness, and he never wanted one. Then he met Gerda, and they brought Paavo into their lives.

He realized that families *were* a weakness, but they were a strength as well.

And he was going to make sure his was safe, no matter what it took.

9

It had taken more work than Broduer expected to get the body back to the coroner's office. Just to get the stupid crate out of the warehouse, he'd had to sign documentation swearing he wouldn't use it to make money at the expense of Ansel Management.

"Company policy," Najib Ansel had said with an insincere smile.

If Broduer hadn't known better, he would have thought that Ansel was just trying to make things difficult for him.

But things had become difficult for Broduer when DeRicci's partner, Rayvon Lake, arrived. Lake had been as angry as Broduer had ever seen him, claiming that DeRicci—who was apparently a junior officer to Lake—had been giving him orders.

Lake had shouted at everyone, except Broduer. Broduer had fended a shouting match off by holding up his hands and saying, "I'm not sure what killed this girl, but I don't like it. It might contaminate everything. We have to get her out of here, now."

Lake, who was a notorious germophobe (which Broduer found strange in a detective), had gulped and stepped back. Broduer had gotten the crate to the warehouse door before Ansel had come after him with all the documentation crap.

Maybe Ansel had done it just so that he wouldn't have to talk with Lake. Broduer would have done anything to avoid Lake—and apparently just had.

Broduer smiled to himself, relieved to be back at the coroner's office. The office was a misnomer—the coroners had their own building, divided into sections to deal with the various kinds of death that happened in Armstrong.

Broduer had tested out of the alien section after two years of trying. He hated working in an environmental suit, like he so often had to. Weirdly (he always thought) humans started in the alien section and had to get a promotion to work on human cadavers. Probably because no one really wanted to see the interior of a Sequev more than once. No human did, anyway.

There were more than a dozen alien coroners, most of whom worked with human supervisors since many alien cultures did not investigate cause of death. Armstrong was a human-run society on a human-run Moon, so human laws applied here, and human laws always needed a cause of death.

Broduer had placed Sonja Mycenae on the autopsy table, carefully positioning her before beginning work, and he'd been startled at how well proportioned she was.

Most people had obvious flaws, at least when a coroner was looking at them. One arm a little too long, a roll of fat under the chin, a misshapen ankle.

He hadn't removed her clothing yet, but as far as he could tell from the work he'd done with her already, nothing was unusual.

Which made her unusual all by herself.

He also couldn't see any obvious cause of death. He had noted, however, that full rigor mortis had already set in. Which was odd, since the decomposition, according to the exam his nanobots had already started, seemed to have progressed at a rate that put her death at least five hours earlier.

By now, under the conditions she'd been stored in, she should have still been pliable—at least her limbs. Rigor began in the eyes, jaw, and neck then spread to the face and through the chest before getting to the limbs. The fingers and toes were always the last to stiffen up.

That made him suspicious, particularly since livor mortis also seemed off.

He would have thought, given how long she had been curled inside that crate, that the blood would have pooled in the side of her body resting on top of the compost heap. But no blood had pooled at all.

He had bots move the autopsy table into one of the more advanced autopsy theaters. He wanted every single device he could find to do the work.

He suspected she'd been killed with some kind of hardening poison. They had become truly popular with assassins in the last two decades, and had just recently been banned from the Moon. Hardening poisons killed quickly by absorbing all the liquid in the body and/or by baking it into place.

It was a quick death, but a painful one, and usually the victim's muscles froze in place, so she couldn't even express that pain as it occurred.

He put on a high-grade environmental suit in an excess of caution. Some of the hardening poisons leaked out of the pores and then infected anyone who touched them.

What he had to determine was if Sonja Mycenae had died of one of those, and if her body had been placed in a waste crate not just to hide the corpse, but to infect the food supply in Armstrong.

Because the Growing Pits inspections looked at the growing materials—the soil, the water, the light, the atmosphere, and the seeds. The inspectors would also look at the fertilizer, but if it came from a certified organization like Ansel Management, then there would only be a cursory search of materials.

Hardening poisons could thread their way into the DNA of a plant—just a little bit, so that, say, an apple wouldn't be quite as juicy. A little hardening poison wouldn't really hurt the fruit of a tree (although that tree might eventually die of what a botanist would consider a wasting disease), but a trace of hardening poison in the human system would have an impact over time. And if the human continued to eat things with hardening poisons in them, the poisons would build up, until the body couldn't take it any more.

A person poisoned in that way wouldn't die like Sonja Mycenae had; instead, the poison would overwhelm the standard nanohealers that everyone had installed, that person would get sick, and organs would slowly fail. Armstrong would have a plague but not necessarily know what caused it.

He double-checked his gloves, then let out a breath. Yes, he knew he was being paranoid. But he thought about these things a lot—the kinds of death that could happen with just a bit of carelessness, like sickness in a dome, poison through the food supply, the wrong mix in the air supply.

He had moved from working with living humans to working with the dead primarily because his imagination was so vivid. Usually working with the dead calmed him. The regular march of unremarkable deaths reminded him that most people would die of natural causes after 150 or more years, maybe longer if they took good care of themselves.

Working with the dead usually gave him hope.

But Sonja Mycenae was making him nervous.

And he didn't like that at all.

10

DESHIN HAD JUST finished talking with Gerda when Koos sent him an encoded message:

Need to talk as soon as you can.

Now's fine, Deshin sent.

He moved away from the windows, where he'd been standing as he made sure Gerda was okay. She actually sounded happy, which she hadn't since Paavo moved in.

She said she no longer felt like her every move was being judged.

Paavo seemed happier too. He wasn't crying as much, and he didn't cling as hard to Gerda. Instead, he played with a mobile from his bouncy chair and watched her cook, cooing most of the time.

Just that one report made Deshin feel like he had made the right choice with Sonja.

Not that he had had a doubt—at least about her—after her reaction that morning. But apparently a tiny doubt had lingered about whether or not he and Gerda needed the help of a nanny.

Gerda's report on Paavo's calmness eased that. Deshin knew they would have hard times ahead—he wasn't deluding himself—but he also knew that they had made the right choice to go nanny-free.

He hadn't told Gerda what happened to Sonja, and he wouldn't, until he knew more. He didn't want to spoil Gerda's day.

The door to Deshin's office opened, and Koos entered, looking upset. "Upset" was actually the wrong word. Something about Koos made Deshin think the man was afraid.

Then Deshin shook that thought off: he'd seen Koos in extremely dangerous circumstances and the man had never seemed afraid.

"I did what you asked," Koos said without preamble. "I started vetting her all over again."

Deshin leaned against the desk, just like he had done when he spoke to Sonja. "And?"

"Her employers on Earth are still filing updates about her exemplary work for them."

Deshin felt a chill. "Tell me that they were just behind in their reports."

Koos shook his head. "She's still working for them."

"How is that possible?" Deshin asked. "We vetted her. We even used a DNA sample to make sure her DNA was the same as the DNA on file with the service. And we collected it ourselves."

Koos swallowed. "We used the service's matching program."

"Of course we did," Deshin said. "They were the ones with the DNA on file."

"We could have requested that sample, and then run it ourselves."

That chill Deshin had felt became a full-fledged shiver. "What's the difference?"

"Depth," Koos said. "They don't go into the same kind of depth we would go into in our search. They just look at standard markers, which is really all most people would need to confirm identity."

His phrasing made Deshin uncomfortable. "She's not who she said she was?"

Koos let out a small sigh. "It's more complicated than that."

More complicated. Deshin shifted. He could only think of one thing that would be more complicated.

Sonja was a clone.

And that created all kinds of other issues.

But first, he had to confirm his suspicion.

"You checked for clone marks, right?" Deshin asked. "I know you did. We always do."

The Earth Alliance required human clones to have a mark on the back of their neck or behind their ear that gave their number. If they were the second clone from an original, the number would be "2."

Clones also did not have birth certificates. They had day of creation documents. Deshin had a strict policy for Deshin Enterprises: every person he hired had to have a birth certificate or a document showing that they, as a clone, had been legally adopted by an original human and therefore could be considered human under the law.

When it came to human clones, Earth Alliance and Armstrong laws were the same: clones were property. They were created and owned by their creator. They could be bought or sold, and they had no rights of their own. The law did not distinguish between slow-grow clones, which were raised like any naturally born human child, and fast-grow clones, which reached full adult size in days, but never had a full-grown human intelligence.

The laws were an injustice, but only clones seemed to protest it, and they, as property, had no real standing.

Koos's lips thinned. He didn't answer right away.

Deshin cursed. He hated having clones in his business, and didn't own any, even though he could take advantage of the loopholes in the law.

Clones made identity theft too easy, and made an organization vulnerable.

He always made certain his organization remained protected.

Or he had, until now.

"We did check like we do with all new hires." Koos's voice was strangled. "And we also checked her birth certificate. It was all in order."

"But now you're telling me it's not," Deshin said.

Koos's eyes narrowed a little, not with anger, but with tension.

"The first snag we hit," he said, "was that we were not able to get Sonja Mycenae's DNA from the service. According to them, she's currently employed, and not available for hire, so the standard service-subsidized searches are inactive. She likes her job. I looked: the job is the old one, not the one with you."

Deshin crossed his arms. "If that's the case, then how did we get the service comparison in the first place?"

"At first, I worried that someone had spoofed our system," Koos said. "It hadn't. There was a redundancy in the service's files that got repaired. I checked with a tech at the service. The tech said they'd been hit with an attack that replicated everything inside their system. It lasted for about two days."

"Let me guess," Deshin said. "Two days around the point we'd hired Sonja."

Koos nodded.

"I'm amazed the tech admitted it," Deshin said.

"It wasn't their glitch," Koos said. "It happened because of some government program."

"Government?" Deshin asked.

"The Earth Alliance required some changes in their software," Koos said. "They made the changes and the glitch appeared. The service caught it, removed the Earth Alliance changes, and petitioned to return to their old way of doing things. Their petition was granted."

Deshin couldn't sit still with this. "Did Sonja know this glitch was going to happen?"

Koos shrugged. "I don't know what she knew."

Deshin let out a small breath. He felt a little off-balance. "I assume the birth certificate was stolen."

"It was real. We checked it. I double-checked it today," Koos said.

Deshin rubbed his forehead. "So, was the Sonja Mycenae I hired a clone or is the clone at the other job? Or does Sonja Mycenae have a biological twin?"

Koos looked down, which was all the answer Deshin needed. She was a clone.

"She left a lot of DNA this morning," Koos said. "Tears, you name it. We checked it all."

Deshin waited, even though he knew.

He knew, and he was getting furious.

"She had no clone mark," Koos said, "except in her DNA. The telomeres were marked."

"Designer Criminal Clone," Deshin said. A number of criminal organizations, most operating outside the Alliance, made and trained Designer Criminal Clones for just the kind of thing that had happened to Deshin.

The clone, who replicated someone the family or the target knew casually, would slide into a business or a household for months, maybe years, and steal information. Then the clone would leave with that information on a chip, bringing it to whoever had either hired that DCC or who had grown and trained the clone.

"I don't think she was a DCC," Koos said. "The markers don't fit anyone we know."

"A new player?" Deshin asked.

Koos shrugged. Then he took one step forward. "I'm going to check everything she touched, everything she did, sir. But this is my error, and it's a serious one. It put your business and more importantly your family in danger. I know you're going to fire me, but before you do, let me track down her creator. Let me redeem myself."

Deshin didn't move for a long moment. He had double-checked everything Koos had done. *Everything*. Because Sonja Mycenae—or whatever that clone was named—was going to work in his home, with his family.

"Do you think she stole my son's DNA?" Deshin asked quietly.

"I don't know. Clearly she didn't have any with her today, but if she had handlers—"

"She wouldn't have had trouble meeting them, because Gerda and I didn't want a live-in nanny." Deshin cursed silently. There was more than enough blame to go around, and if he were honest with himself, most of it belonged to him. He had been so concerned with raising his son, that he hadn't taken the usual precautions in protecting his family.

"I would like to retrace all of her steps," Koos said. "We might be able to find her handler."

"Or not," Deshin said. The handler had killed her the moment she had ceased to be useful. The handler felt he could waste a slow-grow clone, expensive and well-trained, placed in the household of a man everyone believed to be a criminal mastermind.

Some mastermind. He had screwed up something this important.

He bit back anger, not sure how he would tell Gerda. *If* he would tell Gerda.

Something had been planned here, something he hadn't figured out yet, and that planning was not complete. Sonja (or whatever her name was) had confirmed that with her reaction to her dismissal. She was terrified, and she probably knew she was going to die.

He sighed.

"I will quit now if you'd like me to," Koos said.

Deshin wasn't ready to fire Koos.

"Find out who she answered to. Better yet, find out who made her," Deshin said. "Find her handler. We'll figure out what happens to you after you complete that assignment."

Koos nodded, but didn't thank Deshin. Koos knew his employer well, knew that the thanks would only irritate him.

Deshin hated to lose Koos, but Koos was no longer 100% trustworthy. He should have caught this. He should have tested Sonja's DNA himself.

And that was why Deshin would put new security measures into place for his business and his family. Measures he designed.

He'd also begin the search for the new head of security. It would take time.

And, he was afraid, it would take time to find out what exactly Sonja (or whatever her name was) had been trying to do inside his home.

That had just become his first priority.

Because no one was going to hurt his family.

No matter what he had to do to protect them.

11

BRODUER HAD SIX different nanoprobes digging into various places on the dead woman's skin, when a holographic computer screen appeared in front of him, a red warning light flashing.

He moaned slightly. He hated the lights. They got sent to his boss automatically, and often the damn lights reported something he had done wrong.

Well, not wrong, exactly, but not according to protocol.

The irony was, everything he had done in this autopsy so far had been exactly according to protocol.

The body was on an isolated gurney, which was doing its own investigation; they were in one of the most protected autopsy chambers in the coroner's office; and Broduer was using all the right equipment.

He even had on the right environmental suit for the type of poison he suspected killed the woman.

He cursed, silently and creatively, wishing he could express his frustration aloud, but knowing he couldn't, because it would become part of the permanent record.

Instead, he glared at the light and wished it would go away. Not that he could make it go away with a look.

The light had a code he had never seen before. He put his gloved finger on the code, and it created a whole new screen.

This body is cloned. Please file the permissions code to autopsy this clone or cease work immediately.

"The hell…?" he asked, then realized he had spoken aloud, and he silently cursed himself. Some stupid supervisor, reviewing the footage, would think he was too dumb to know a cloned body from a real body.

But he had made a mistake. He hadn't taken DNA in the field. He had used facial recognition to identify this woman, and he had told DeRicci who the woman was based not on the DNA testing, but on the facial recognition.

Of course, if DeRicci hadn't pressed him to give her an identification right away, he would have followed procedure.

Broduer let out a small sigh, then remembered what he had been doing.

There was still a way to cover his ass. He had been investigating whether or not this woman died of a hardening poison, and if that poison had gotten into the composting system.

He would use that as his excuse, and then mention that he needed to continue to find cause of death for public health reasons.

Besides, someone should want to know who was killing clones and putting them into the composting.

Not that it was illegal, exactly. After all, a dead clone was organic waste, just like rotted vegetables were.

He shuddered, not wanting to think about it. Maybe someone should tell the Armstrong City Council to ban the composting of any human flesh be it original or cloned.

He sighed. He didn't want to be the one to do it. He'd slip the suggestion into his supervisor's ear and hope that she would take him up on it.

He pinged his supervisor, telling her that it was important she contact him right away.

Then he bent over the body, determined to get as much work done as possible before someone shut this investigation down entirely.

12

DeRicci sat in her car in the part of Armstrong Police Department Parking Lot set aside for detectives. She hadn't used the car all day, but it was the most private place she could think of to watch the footage Deshin had given her.

She didn't want to take the footage inside the station until she'd had a chance to absorb it. She wasn't sure how relevant it was, and she wasn't sure what her colleagues would think of it.

Or, if she were being truthful with herself, she didn't want Lake anywhere near this thing. He had some dubious connections, and he might just confiscate the footage—not for the case, but for reasons she didn't really want to think about.

So, she stayed in her car, quietly watching the footage for the second time, taking mental notes. Because something was off here. People rarely got that upset getting fired from a job, at least not in front of a man known to be as dangerous as Luc Deshin.

Besides, he had handled the whole thing well, made it sound like not a firing, more like something inevitable, something that Sonja Mycenae's excellent job performance helped facilitate.

The man was impressive, although DeRicci would never admit that to anyone else.

When DeRicci watched the footage the first time, she had been amazed at how calmly Deshin handled Mycenae's meltdown. He managed to stay out of her way, and he managed to get his security into the office without making her get even worse.

Not that it would be easy for her to be worse. If De-Ricci hadn't known that Sonja Mycenae was murdered shortly after this footage was taken, DeRicci would have thought the woman unhinged. Instead, DeRicci knew that Mycenae was terrified.

She had known that losing her position would result in something awful, mostly likely her death.

But why? And what did someone have on a simple nanny with no record, something bad enough to get her to work in the home of a master criminal and his wife, bad enough to make her beg said criminal to keep the job?

DeRicci didn't like this. She particularly did not like the way that Mycenae disappeared off the security footage as she stepped outside of the building. She stood beside the building and sobbed for a few minutes, then staggered away.

No nearby buildings had exterior security cameras, and what DeRicci could get from the street cameras told her little.

Um, Detective?

DeRicci sighed. The contact came from Broduer, on her links. He was asking for a visual, which she was not inclined to give him.

But he probably had something to show her from the autopsy.

So she activated the visual, in two dimensions, making his head float above the car's control panel. Broduer wore an environmental suit, but he had removed the hood that had covered his face. It hung behind his skull like a half-visible alien appendage.

News for me, Ethan? she asked, hoping to move him along quickly. He could get much too chatty for her tastes.

Well, you're not going to like any of it. He ran a hand through his hair, messing it up. It looked a little damp, as if he'd been sweating inside the suit.

DeRicci waited. She didn't know how she could like or dislike any news about the woman's death. It was a case. A sad and strange case, but a case nonetheless.

She died from a hardening poison, Broduer sent. *I've narrowed it down to one of five related types. I'm running the test now to see which poison it actually is.*

Poison. That took effort. Not in the actual application—many poisons were impossible to see, taste, or feel—but in the planning.

Someone wanted this woman dead, and then they wanted to keep her death secret.

That's a weird way to kill someone, DeRicci sent.

Broduer looked concerned. Over the woman? He usually saw corpses as a curiosity, not as someone to empathize with.

That was one of the few things DeRicci liked about Broduer. He could handle a job as a job.

It is *a weird way to kill someone,* Broduer sent. Then he glanced over his shoulder as if he expected someone to enter his office and yell at him. *The thing is, one of these types of poisons could contaminate the food supply.*

What? she sent. Or maybe she said that out loud. Or both. She felt cold. Contaminate the food supply? With a body?

She wasn't quite sure of the connection, but she didn't like it.

She hadn't liked the corpse in the compost part of this case from the very first.

Broduer took an obvious deep breath and his gaze met hers. She stabilized the floating image, so she wasn't tracking him as he moved up, down, and across the control panel.

If, he sent, *the poison leaked from the skin and got into the compost, then it would be layered onto the growing plants, which would take in the poison along with the nutrients. It wouldn't be enough to kill anyone, unless someone'd been doing this for a long time.*

DeRicci shook her head. *Then I don't get it. How is this anything other than a normal contamination?*

If a wannabe killer wants to destroy the food supply, he'd do stuff like this for months, Broduer sent. *People would start dying mysteriously. Generally, the old and the sick would go first, or people who are vulnerable in the parts of their bodies this stuff targets.*

Wouldn't the basic nanohealers take care of this problem? DeRicci was glad they weren't doing this verbally. She didn't want him to know how shaken she was.

If it were small or irregular, sure, he sent. *But over time? No. They're not made to handle huge contaminations. They're not even designed to recognize these kinds of poisons. That's why these poisons can kill so quickly.*

DeRicci suppressed a shudder.

Great, she sent. *How do we investigate food contamination like that?*

That's your problem, Detective, Broduer sent back, somewhat primly. *I'd suggest starting with a search of records, seeing if there has been a rise in deaths in vulnerable populations.*

Can't you do that easier than I can? She sent, even though she knew he would back out. It couldn't hurt to try to get him to help.

Not at the moment, he sent, *I have a job to do.*

She nearly cursed at him. But she managed to control herself. A job to do. The bastard. *She* had a job to do too, and it was just as important as his job.

This was why she hated working with Broduer. He was a jerk.

Well, she sent, *let me know the type of poison first, before I get into that part of the investigation. You said there were five, and only one could contaminate the food supply. You think that's the one we're dealing with?*

I don't know yet, Detective, he sent. *I'll know when the testing is done.*

Which will take how long?

He shrugged. *Not long, I hope.*

Great, she sent again. She wanted to push him, but pushing him sometimes made him even more passive/ aggressive about getting work done.

Well, you were right, she sent. *I didn't like it. Now I'm off to investigate even more crap.*

Um, not yet, Broduer sent.

Not yet? Who was this guy and why did he think he could control everything she did. She clenched her fists. Pretty soon, she would tell this idiot exactly what she thought of him, and that wouldn't make for a good working relationship.

Um, yeah, he sent. *There's one other problem.*

She waited, her fists so tight her fingernails were digging into the skin of her palm.

He looked down. *I, um, misidentified your woman.*

You what? He had been an idiot about helping her, and then he told her that he had done crappy work?

This man was the absolutely worst coroner she'd ever worked with (which was saying something) and she was going to report him to the Chief of Detectives, maybe even to the Chief of Police, and get him removed from his position.

Yeah, Broduer sent. *She's, um, not Sonja Mycenae.*

You said that, DeRicci sent. Already, her mind was racing. Misidentifying the corpse would cause all kinds of problems, not the least of which would be problems with Luc Deshin. *Who the hell is she, then?*

Broduer's skin had turned gray. He clearly knew he had screwed up big time. *She's a clone of Sonja Mycenae.*

A what? DeRicci rolled her eyes. That would have been good to know right from the start. Because it meant the investigation had gone in the wrong direction from the moment she had a name.

A clone. I'm sorry, Detective.

You should be, DeRicci sent. *I shouldn't even be on this investigation This isn't a homicide.*

Well, technically, it's the same thing, Broduer sent.

Technically, it isn't, DeRicci sent. She'd had dozens of clone cases before, and no matter how much she argued with the Chief of Detectives, Andrea Gumiela, it didn't matter. The clones weren't human under the law; their deaths fell into property crimes, generally vandalism or destruction of valuable property, depending on how much the clone was worth or how much it cost to create.

But, Detective, she's a human being…

DeRicci sighed. She believed that, but what she believed didn't matter. What mattered was what the law said and how her boss handled it. And she'd been through this with Gumiela. Gumiela would send DeRicci elsewhere.

Gumiela hadn't seen the poor girl crying and begging for her life in front of Deshin. Gumiela hadn't seen the near-perfect corpse, posed as if she were sleeping on a pile of compost.

Wait a minute, DeRicci sent. *You told me about the poisoning first because…?*

Because, Detective, she might not be human, but she might have been a weapon or weaponized material. And that would fall into your jurisdiction, wouldn't it?

Just when she thought that Broduer was the worst person she had ever worked with, he manipulated a clone case to keep it inside DeRicci's Detective Division.

I don't determine jurisdiction, she sent, mostly because this was on the record, and she didn't want to show her personal feelings on something that might hit court and derail any potential prosecution.

But check, would you? Broduer sent. *Because someone competent should handle this.*

She wasn't sure what "this" was: the dead clone or the contamination.

Just send me all the information, DeRicci sent, *and let me know the minute you confirm which hardening poison killed this clone.*

I'll have it soon, Broduer sent and signed off.

DeRicci leaned back in the car seat, her cheeks warm. She had gone to Luc Deshin for nothing.

Or had she?

Which Sonja Mycenae had Deshin fired that morning? The real one? Or the clone?

DeRicci let herself out of the car. She had to talk to Gumiela. But before she did, she needed to find out where the real Mycenae was—and fast.

13

DESHIN WASN'T CERTAIN how to tell Gerda that Sonja had been a plant, placed in their home for a reason he didn't know yet.

He wandered his office, screens moving with him as he examined the tracker he had placed in Sonja. Then he winced. Every time he thought of the clone as Sonja, he felt like a fool. From now on, he would just call her the clone, because she clearly wasn't Sonja.

So he examined the information from the tracker he had placed in the clone's palm the moment she was hired. She hadn't known he had inserted it. He had done it when he shook her hand, using technology that didn't show up on any of the regular scans.

He wished he had been paranoid enough to install a video tracker, but he had thought—or rather, Gerda had thought—that their nanny needed her privacy in her off time.

Of course, that had been too kind. Deshin should have tracked the clone the way he tracked anyone he didn't entirely trust.

Whenever the clone had been with Paavo, Deshin had always kept a screen open. He'd even set an alert in case the clone took Paavo out of the house without Gerda accompanying them. That alert had never activated, because Gerda had always been nearby when the clone was with Paavo.

Deshin was grateful for that caution now. He had no idea what serious crisis they had dodged.

He was now searching through all the other information in the tracker—where the clone had gone during her days off, where she had spent her free time. He knew that Koos had been, in theory, making sure she had no unsavory contacts—or at least, Deshin had tasked Koos with doing that.

Now, Deshin was double-checking his head of security, making certain that he had actually done his job.

The first thing Deshin had done was make certain that the clone hadn't gone to the bad parts of town. According to the tracker, she hadn't. Her apartment was exactly where she had claimed it was, and as far as he could tell, all she had done in her off hours was shop for her own groceries, eaten at a local restaurant, and gone home.

He had already sent a message to one of the investigative services he used. He wanted them to search the clone's apartment. He wanted video and DNA and all kinds of trace. He wanted an investigation of her finances and a look at the things she kept.

He also didn't want anyone from Deshin Enterprises associated with that search. He knew that his investigative service would keep him out of it. They had done so before.

He had hired them to search before he had known she was a clone. He had hired them while he was waiting for his attorney to look at the footage he had given that detective.

With luck, they'd be done with the search by now.

But he had decided to check the tracker himself, looking for anomalies.

The only anomaly he had found was a weekly visit to a building in downtown Armstrong. On her day off, she went to that building at noon. She had also been at that building the evening Deshin had hired her.

He scanned the address, looking for the businesses that rented or owned the place. The building had dozens of small offices, and none of the businesses were registered with the city.

He found that odd: usually the city insisted that every business register for tax purposes.

So he traced the building's ownership. He went through several layers of corporate dodges to find something odd: the building's owner wasn't a corporation at all.

It was the Earth Alliance.

He let out a breath, and then sank into a nearby chair.

Suddenly everything made sense.

The Earth Alliance had been after him for years, convinced he was breaking a million different Alliance laws and not only getting away with it, but making billions from the practice.

Ironically, he had broken a lot of Alliance laws when he started out, and he still had a lot of sketchy associates, but *he* hadn't broken a law in years and years.

Still, it would have been a coup for someone in Alliance government to bring down Luc Deshin and his criminal enterprises.

The Alliance had found it impossible to plant listening devices and trackers in Deshin's empire. The Alliance was always behind Deshin Enterprises when it came to technology. And Deshin himself was innately cautious—

Or he had thought he was, until this incident with the clone.

They had slipped her into his home. They might have had a hundred purposes in doing so—as a spy on his family, to steal familial DNA, to set up tracking equipment in a completely different way than it had been done before.

And for an entire month, they had been successful.

He was furious at himself, but he knew he couldn't let that emotion dominate his thoughts. He had to take action, and he had to do so now.

He used his links to summon Ishiyo Cumija to his office. He'd been watching her for some time. She hadn't been Koos's second in command in the security department. She had set up her own fiefdom, and once she had mentioned to Deshin that she worried no one was taking security seriously enough.

At the time, he had thought she was making a play for Koos's job. Deshin *still* thought she was making a play for Koos's job on that day, but she might have been doing so with good reason.

Now, she would get a chance to prove herself.

While Deshin waited for her, he checked the clone's DNA and found that strange clone mark embedded into her system. He had never seen anything like it either. The Designer Criminal Clones he'd run into had always had a product stamp embedded into their DNA. This wasn't a standard DCC product stamp.

It looked like something else.

He copied it, then opened Cumija's file, accessed the DNA samples she had to give every week, and searched to see if there was any kind of mark. His system always searched for the DCC product stamps, but rarely searched for other examples of cloning, including shortened telomeres.

Shortened telomeres could happen naturally. In the past, he'd found that searching for them gave him so many false positives—staff members who were older than they appeared, employees who had had serious injuries—that he decided to stop searching for anything but the product marks.

He wondered now if that had been a mistake.

His search of Cumija's DNA found no DCC product mark, and nothing matching the mark his system had found in the clone's DNA.

As the search ended, Cumija entered the office.

She was stunningly beautiful, with a cap of straight hair so black it almost looked blue, and dancing black eyes. Until he met Cumija, he would never have thought that someone so very attractive would function well in a security position, but she had turned out to be one of his best bodyguards.

She dressed like a woman sexually involved with a very rich man. Her clothing always revealed her taut nut-brown skin and her fantastic legs. Sometimes she looked nearly naked in the clothing she had chosen. Men and women watched her wherever she went, and dismissed her as someone decorative, someone being used.

On this day, she wore a white dress that crossed her breasts with an X, revealing her sides, and expanding to cover her hips and buttocks. Her matching white shoes looked as deadly as the shoes that she had used to kill a man trying to get to Deshin one afternoon.

"That nanny we hired turns out to have been a clone," Deshin said without greeting.

"Yes, I heard." Cumija's voice was low and sexy in keeping with her appearance.

"Has Koos made an announcement?" Deshin asked. Because he would have recommended against it.

"No," she said curtly, and Deshin almost smiled. She monitored everything Koos did. It was a great trait in a security officer, a terrible trait in a subordinate—at least from the perspective of someone in Koos's position.

Deshin said, "I need you to check the other employees—*you*, and you *only*. I don't want anyone to know what you're doing. I have the marker that was in the cloned Sonja Mycenae's DNA. I want you to see if there's a match. I also want a secondary check for Designer Criminal Clone marks, and then I want you to do a slow search of anyone with abnormal telomeres."

Cumija didn't complain, even though he was giving her a lot of work. "You want me to check everyone," she said.

"Yes," he said. "Start with people who have access to me, and then move outward. Do it quickly and quietly."

"Yes, sir," she said.

"Report the results directly to me," he said.

"All right," she said. "Are links all right?"

"No," he said. "You will report in person."

She nodded, thanked him, and left the office.

He stood there for a moment, feeling a little shaken. If the Alliance was trying to infiltrate his organization, then he wouldn't be surprised if there were other clones stationed in various areas, clones he had missed.

After Cumija checked, he would have Koos do the same check, and see if he came up with the same result.

Deshin went back to his investigation of that building that the clone had visited regularly. He had no firm evidence of Earth Alliance involvement. Just suspicions, at least at the moment.

And regular citizens of the Alliance would be stunned to think that their precious Alliance would infiltrate businesses using slow-grow clones, and then disposing of them when they lost their usefulness.

But Deshin knew the Alliance did all kinds of extra-legal things to protect itself over the centuries. And somewhere, Deshin had been flagged as a threat to the Alliance.

He had known that for some time.

He had always expected some kind of infiltration of his business.

But the infiltration of his home was personal.

And it needed to stop.

14

ETHAN BRODUER LOOKED at the information pouring across his screen, and let out a sigh of relief.

The hardening poison wasn't one of the kinds that could leach through the skin. He still had to test the compost to see if the poison had contaminated it, but he doubted that.

The livor mortis told him that she had died elsewhere, and then been placed in the crate. And given how fast this hardening poison acted, the blood wouldn't have been able to pool for more than a few minutes anyway.

He stood and walked back into the autopsy room. Now that he knew the woman had died of something that wouldn't hurt him if he came in contact with her skin or breathed the air around her, he didn't need the environmental suit.

Hers was the only body in this autopsy room. He had placed her on her back before sending the nano-bots into her system. They were still working, finding out even more about her.

He knew now that she was a slow-grow clone, which meant she had lived some twenty years, had hopes, dreams, and desires. As a forensic pathologist who had examined hundreds of human corpses—cloned and non-cloned—the *only* difference he had ever seen were the telomeres and the clone marks.

Slow-grow clones were human beings in everything but the law.

He could make the claim that fast-grow clones were too, that they had the mind of a child inside an adult body, but he tried not to think about that one. Because it meant that all those horrors visited on fast-grow clones meant those horrors were visited on a human being that hadn't seen more than a few years of life, an innocent in all possible ways.

He blinked hard, trying not to think about any of it. Then he stopped beside her table. Lights moved along the back of it, different beams examining her, trying to glean her medical history and every single story her biology could tell.

Now that it was clear that the poison which killed her wouldn't contaminate the dome, no one would investigate this case. No one would care.

No one legally *had* to care.

He sighed, then shook his head, wondering if he could make one final push to solve her murder.

Detective DeRicci had asked for a list of bodies found in the crates. Broduer would make her that list after all, but before he did, he would see if those bodies were "human" or clones.

If they were clones, then there was a sabotage problem, some kind of property crime—hell, it wasn't his job to come up with the charge, not when he gave her the thing to investigate.

But maybe he could find something to investigate, something that would have the side benefit of giving some justice to this poor woman, lying alone and unwanted on his autopsy table.

"I'm doing what I can," he whispered, and then wished he hadn't spoken aloud.

His desire to help her would be in the official record. Then he corrected himself: There would be no official record, since she wasn't officially a murder victim.

He was so sorry about that. He'd still document everything he could. Maybe in the future, the laws would change.

Maybe in the future, her death would matter as more than a statistic.

Maybe, in the future, she'd be recognized as a person, instead of something to be thrown away, like leftover food.

15

THE CHIEF OF DETECTIVES, Andrea Gumiela, had an office one floor above DeRicci's, but it was light years from DeRicci's. DeRicci's office was in the center of a large room, sectioned off with dark movable walls. She could protect her area by putting a bubble around it for a short period of time, particularly if she were conducting an interview that she felt wouldn't work in one of the interview rooms, but there was no real privacy and no sense of belonging.

DeRicci hated working out in the center, and hoped that one day she would eventually get an office of her own.

The tiny aspirations of the upwardly mobile, her ex-husband would have said. She couldn't entirely disagree. He had the unfortunate habit of being right.

And as she looked at Gumiela's office, which took up much of the upper floor, DeRicci knew she would never achieve privacy like this. She wasn't political enough.

Some days she felt like she was one infraction away from being terminated.

Most days, she didn't entirely care.

Andrea Gumiela, on the other hand, was the most political person DeRicci had ever met. Her office was designed so that it wouldn't offend anyone. It didn't have artwork on the walls, nor did it have floating imagery. The décor shifted colors when someone from outside the department entered.

When someone was as unimportant as DeRicci, the walls were a neutral beige, and the desk a dark woodlike color. The couch and chairs at the far end of the room matched the desk.

But DeRicci had been here when the Governor-General arrived shortly after her election, and the entire room shifted to vibrant colors—the purples and whites associated with the Governor-General herself.

The shift, which happened as the Governor-General was announced, had disturbed DeRicci, but Gumiela managed it as a matter of course. She was going to get promoted some day, and she clearly hoped the Governor-General would do it.

"Make it fast," Gumiela said as DeRicci entered. "I have meetings all afternoon."

Gumiela was tall and heavyset, but her black suit made her look thinner than she was—probably with some kind of tech that DeRicci didn't want to think about. Gumiela's red hair was piled on top of her head, making her long face seem even longer.

"I wanted to talk with you in person about that woman we found in the Ansel Management crate," DeRicci said.

Gumiela, for all her annoying traits, did keep up on the investigations.

"I thought Rayvon Lake was in charge of that case," Gumiela said.

DeRicci shrugged. "He's not in charge of anything, sir. Honestly, when it comes to cases like this, I don't even like to consult him."

Gumiela studied her. "He's your partner, Detective."

"Maybe," DeRicci said, "but he doesn't investigate crimes. He takes advantage of them."

"That's quite a charge," Gumiela said.

"I can back it with evidence," DeRicci said.

"Do so," Gumiela said, to DeRicci's surprise. DeRicci frowned. Had Gumiela paired them so that DeRicci would bring actual evidence against Lake to the Chief's office? It made an odd kind of sense. No one could control Lake, and no one could control DeRicci, but for different reasons.

Lake had his own tiny fiefdom, and DeRicci was just plain contrary.

"All right," DeRicci said, feeling a little off balance. She hadn't expected anything positive from Gumiela.

And then Gumiela reverted to type. "I'm in a hurry, remember?"

"Yes, sir, sorry, sir," DeRicci said. This woman always set her teeth on edge. "The woman in the crate, she was killed with a hardening poison. For a while, Broduer thought she might have been put there to contaminate the food supply, but it was the wrong kind of poison. We're okay on that."

Gumiela raised her eyebrows slightly. Apparently she hadn't heard about the possible contamination. De-Ricci had been worried that she had.

"Good…" Gumiela said in a tone that implied …*and…*?

"But, I got a list from him, and sir, someone is dumping bodies in those crates all over the city, and has been for at least a year, maybe more."

"No one saw this pattern?" Gumiela asked.

"The coroner's office noticed it," DeRicci said, making sure she kept her voice calm. "Ansel Management noticed it, but the owner, Najib Ansel, tells me that over the decades his family has owned the business, they've seen all kinds of things dumped in the crates."

"Bodies, though, bodies should have caught our attention," Gumiela said. Clearly, DeRicci had Gumiela's attention now.

"No," DeRicci said. "The coroner got called in, but no one called us."

"Well, I'll have to change this," Gumiela said. "I'll—"

"Wait, sir," DeRicci said. "They didn't call us for the correct legal reasons."

Gumiela turned her head slightly, as if she couldn't believe she had heard DeRicci right. "What reasons could those possibly be?"

"The dead are all clones, sir." DeRicci made sure none of her anger showed up in the tone of her voice.

"Clones? Including this one?"

"Yes, sir," DeRicci said. "And they were all apparently slow-grow. If they had been considered human under the law, we would have said they were murdered."

Gumiela let out an exasperated breath. "This woman, this poisoned woman, she's a clone?"

"Yes, sir." DeRicci knew she only had a moment here to convince Gumiela to let her continue on this case. "But I'd like to continue my investigation, sir, because—"

"We'll send it down to property crimes," Gumiela said.

"Sir," DeRicci said. "This pattern suggests a practicing serial killer. At some point, he'll find legal humans, and then he'll be experienced—"

"What is Ansel Management doing to protect its crates?" Gumiela said.

DeRicci felt a small surge of hope. Was Gumiela actually considering this? "They have sensors that locate things by weight and size. They believe they've reported all the bodies that have come through their system in the last several years."

"They believe?" Gumiela asked.

"There's no way to know without checking every crate," DeRicci said.

"Well, this is a health and safety matter. I'll contact the Armstrong City Inspectors and have them investigate all of the recycling/compost plants."

DeRicci tried not to sigh. This wasn't going her way after all. "I think that's a good idea, sir, but—"

"Tell me, Detective," Gumiela said. "Did you have any leads at all on this potential serial before you found out that the bodies belonged to clones?"

DeRicci felt her emotions shift again. She wasn't sure why she was so emotionally involved here. Maybe because she knew no one would investigate, which meant no one would stop this killer, if she couldn't convince Gumiela to keep the investigation in the department.

"She worked as a nanny for Luc Deshin," DeRicci said. "He fired her this morning."

"I thought this was that case," Gumiela said. "His people probably killed her."

"I considered that," DeRicci said. "But he wouldn't have gone through the trouble of firing her if he was just going to kill her."

Gumiela harrumphed. Then she walked around the furniture, trailing her hand over the back of the couch. She was actually considering DeRicci's proposal—and she knew DeRicci had a point.

"Do you know who the original was?" Gumiela asked.

DeRicci's heart sank. She hadn't wanted Gumiela to ask this question. DeRicci hadn't recognized the name, but Lake had. He had left a message on DeRicci's desk—a message that rose up when she touched the desk's surface (the bastard)—which said, *Why do we care that the daughter of an off-Moon crime lord got murdered?*

DeRicci then looked up the Mycenae family. They were a crime family and had been for generations, but Sonja herself didn't seem to be part of the criminal side. She had attended the best schools on Earth, and actually had a nanny certificate. She had renounced her family both visibly and legally, and was trying to live her own life.

"The original's name is Sonja Mycenae," DeRicci said.

"The Mycenae crime family." Gumiela let out a sigh. "There's a pattern here, and one we don't need to be involved in. Obviously there's some kind of winnowing going on in the Earth-Moon crime families. I'll notify the Alliance to watch for something bigger, but I don't think you need to investigate this."

"Sir, I know Luc Deshin thought she was Sonja Mycenae," DeRicci said. "He didn't know she was a clone. That means this isn't a crime family war—"

"We don't know what it is, Detective," Gumiela said. "And despite your obvious interest in the case, I'm moving you off it. I have better things for you to do. I'll send this and the other cases down to Property, and let them handle the investigation."

"Sir, please—"

"Detective, you have plenty to do. I want that report on Rayvon Lake by morning." Gumiela nodded at her.

DeRicci's breath caught. Gumiela was letting her know that if she dropped this case, she might get a new partner. And maybe, she would guarantee that Lake stopped polluting the department.

There was nothing DeRicci could do. This battle was lost.

"Thank you, sir," she said, not quite able to keep the disappointment from her voice.

Gumiela had already returned to her desk.

DeRicci headed for the door. As it opened, Gumiela said, "Detective, one last thing."

DeRicci closed the door and faced Gumiela, expecting some kind of reprimand or some type of admonition.

"Have you done the clone notification?" Gumiela asked.

Earth Alliance law required any official organization that learned of a clone to notify the original, if at all possible.

"Not yet, sir," DeRicci said. She had held off, hoping that she would keep the case. If she had, she could have gone to the Mycenae family, and maybe learned something that had relevance to the case.

"Don't," Gumiela said. "I'll take care of that too."

"I don't mind, sir," DeRicci said.

"The Mycenae require a delicate touch," Gumiela said. "It's better if the notification goes through the most official of channels."

DeRicci nodded. She couldn't quite bring herself to thank Gumiela. Or even to say anything else. So she let herself out of the office.

And stopped in the hallway.

For a moment, she considered going back in and arguing with Gumiela. Because Gumiela wasn't going to notify anyone about the clone. Gumiela probably believed that crime families should fight amongst themselves, so the police didn't have to deal with them.

DeRicci paused for a half second.

If she went back in, she would probably lose her job. Because she would tell Gumiela exactly what she thought of the clone laws, and the way that Property would screw up the investigation, and the fact that *people* were actually dying and being placed in crates.

But, if DeRicci lost her job, she wouldn't be able to investigate anything.

The next time, she got a clone case, she'd sit on that information for as long as she could, finish the investigation, and maybe make an arrest. Sure, it might not hold up, but she could get one of the other divisions to search the perpetrator's home and business, maybe catch him with something else.

This time, she had screwed up. She'd followed the rules too closely. She shouldn't have gone to Gumiela so soon.

DeRicci would know better next time.

And she'd play dumb when Gumiela challenged her over it.

Better to lose a job after solving a case, instead of in the middle of a failed one.

DeRicci sighed. She didn't feel better, but at least she had a plan.

Even if it was a plan she didn't like at all.

16

THE PLACE THAT the clone frequented near the Port was a one-person office, run by a man named Cade Faulke. Ostensibly, Faulke ran an employment consulting office, one that helped people find jobs or training for jobs. But it didn't take a lot of digging to discover that was a cover for a position with Earth Alliance Security.

From what little Deshin could find, it seemed that Faulke worked alone, with an android guard—the kind that usually monitored prisons. Clearly, no one expected Faulke to be investigated: the android alone would have been a tip-off to anyone who looked deeper than the thin cover that Faulke had over his name.

Deshin wondered how many other Earth Alliance operatives worked like that inside of Armstrong. He supposed there were quite a few, monitoring various Earth Alliance projects.

Projects like, apparently, his family.

Deshin let out a sigh. He wandered around his office, feeling like it had become a cage. He clenched and unclenched his fists.

Sometimes he hated the way he had restrained himself to build his business and his family. Sometimes he just wanted to go after someone on his own, squeeze the life out of that person, and then leave the corpse, the way someone had left that clone.

Spying on Deshin's family. Gerda and five-month-old Paavo had done nothing except get involved with him.

And, he would wager, that Sonja Mycenae's family would say the same thing about her.

He stopped. He hadn't spoken to the Mycenae family in a long time, but he owed them for an ancient debt.

He sent an encoded message through his links to Aurla Mycenae, the head of the Mycenae and Sonja's mother, asking for a quick audience.

Then Deshin got a contact from Cumija: *Five low-level employees have the marker. None of them have access to your family or to anything important inside Deshin Enterprises. How do you want me to proceed?*

Send me a list, he sent back.

At that moment, his links chirruped, announcing a massive holomessage so encoded that it nearly overloaded his system. He accepted the message, only to find out it was live.

Aurla Mycenae appeared, full-sized, in the center of his floor. She wore a flowing black gown that accented her dark eyebrows and thick black hair. She had faint lines around her black eyes. Otherwise she looked no older than she had the last time he saw her, at least a decade ago.

"Luc," she said in a throaty voice that hadn't suited her as a young woman, but suited her now. "I get this sense this isn't pleasure."

"No," he said. "I thought I should warn you. I encountered a slow-grow clone of your daughter Sonja."

He decided not to mention that he had hired that clone or that she had been murdered.

Mycenae exhaled audibly. "Damn Earth Alliance. Did they try to embed her in your organization?"

"They succeeded for a time," he said.

"And then?"

So much for keeping the information back. "She turned up dead this morning."

"Typical," Mycenae said. "They've got some kind of operation going, and they've been using clones of my family. You're not the first to tell me this."

"All slow-grow?" Deshin asked.

"Yes," Mycenae said. "We've been letting everyone know that anyone applying for work from our family isn't really from our family. I never thought of contacting you because I thought you went legit."

"I have," Deshin lied. He had gone legit on most things. He definitely no longer had his fingers in the kinds of deals that the Mycenae family was famous for.

"Amazing they tried to embed with you, then," Mycenae said.

"She was nanny to my infant son," he said, and he couldn't quite keep the fury from his voice.

"Oh." Mycenae sighed. "They want to use your family like they're using mine. We're setting something up, Luc. We've got the Alliance division doing this crap tracked, and we're going to shut it down. You want to join us?"

Take on an actual Earth Alliance Division? As a young man, he would have considered it. As a man with a family and a half-legitimate business, he didn't dare take the risk.

"I trust you to handle it, Aurla," he said.

"They have your family's DNA now," she said, clearly as a way of enticement.

"It's of no use to them in the short term," he said, "and by the time we reach the long term, you'll have taken care of everything."

"It's not like you to trust anyone, Luc."

And, back when she had known him well, that had been true. But now, he had to balance security for himself and his business associates with security for his family.

"I'm not trusting you per se, Aurla," he said. "I just know how you operate."

She grinned at him. "I'll let you know when we're done."

"No need," he said. "Good luck."

And then he signed off. The last thing he wanted was to be associated in any way with whatever operation Aurla ran. She was right: it wasn't like him to trust anyone. And while he trusted her to destroy the division that was hurting her family, he didn't trust her to keep him out of it.

Too much contact with Aurla Mycenae, and Deshin might find himself arrested as the perpetrator of whatever she was planning. Mycenae was notorious for betraying colleagues when her back was against the wall.

The list came through his links from Cumija. She was right: the employees were low-level. He didn't recognize any of the names and had to look them up. None of them had even met Deshin.

Getting the clone of Sonja embedded into his family was some kind of coup.

He wouldn't fire anyone yet. He wanted to see if Koos came up with the same list. If he did, then Deshin would move forward.

But these employees were tagged, just like Sonja's clone had been. He decided to see if they had been visiting Faulke as well.

And if they had, Faulke would regret ever crossing paths with Deshin Enterprises.

17

DETECTIVE DERICCI LEFT Andrea Gumiela's office. Gumiela felt herself relax. DeRicci was trouble. She hated rules and she had a sense of righteousness that often made it difficult for her to do her job well. There wasn't a lot of righteousness in the law, particularly when Earth Alliance law trumped Armstrong law.

Gumiela had to balance both.

She resisted the urge to run a hand through her hair. It had taken a lot of work to pile it just so on top of her head, and she didn't like wasting time on her appearance, as important as it was to her job.

Of course, the days when it was important were either days when a major disaster hit Armstrong or when someone in her department screwed up.

She certainly hoped this clone case wouldn't become a screw-up.

She put a hand over her stomach, feeling slightly ill. She had felt ill from the moment DeRicci mentioned Mycenae and Deshin. At that moment, Gumiela knew who had made the clone and who was handling it.

She also knew who was killing the clones—or at least, authorizing the deaths.

DeRicci was right. Those deaths presaged a serial killer (or, in Gumiela's unofficial opinion, already proved one existed). Or worse, the deaths suggested a policy of targeted killings that Gumiela couldn't countenance in her city.

Technically, Gumiela should contact Cade Faulke directly. He had contacted her directly more than once to report a possible upcoming crime. She had used him as an informant, which meant she had used his clones as informants as well.

And those clones were ending up dead.

She choked back bile. Some people, like DeRicci, would say that Gumiela had hands as dirty as Faulke's.

But she hadn't known he was killing the clones when they ceased being useful or when they crossed some line. She also hadn't known that he had been poisoning them using such a painful method. And he hadn't even thought about the possible contamination of the food supply.

Gumiela swallowed hard again, hoping her stomach would settle.

Technically, she should contact him and tell him to cease that behavior.

But Gumiela had been in her job a long time. She knew that telling someone like Faulke to quit was like telling an addict to stop drinking. It wouldn't happen, and it couldn't be done.

She couldn't arrest him either. Even if she caught him in the act, all he was doing was damaging property. And that might get him a fine or two or maybe a year or so in jail, if the clone's owners complained. But if DeRicci was right, the clone's owners were the Earth Alliance itself. And Faulke worked for the Alliance, so technically, *he* was probably the owner, and property owners could do whatever they wanted with their belongings.

Except toss them away in a manner that threatened the public health.

Gumiela sat in one of the chairs and leaned her head back, closing her eyes, forcing herself to think.

She had to do something, and despite what she had said to DeRicci, following procedure was out of the question.

She needed to get Faulke out of Armstrong, only she didn't have the authority to do so.

But she knew who did.

She sat up. Long ago, she'd met Faulke's handler, Ike Jarvis. She could contact him.

Maybe he would work with her.

It was worth a try.

18

OTTO KOOS LED his team to the building housing Cade Faulke's fake business. The building was made of some kind of polymer that changed appearance daily. This day's appearance made it seem like old-fashioned red brick Koos hadn't seen since his childhood on Earth.

Five Ansel Management crates stood in their protected unit in the alley behind the building. They had a cursory lock with a security code that anyone in the building probably had.

It was as much of a confession as he needed.

But the boss would need more. Luc Deshin had given strict orders for this mission—no killing.

Koos knew he was on probation now—maybe forever. He had missed the Mycenae clone, and, after he had done a quick scan of the employees, discovered he had missed at least five others. At least they hadn't been anywhere near the Deshin family.

The Mycenae clone had. Who knew what kind of material the Alliance had gathered?

Faulke knew. Eventually, Koos would know too. It just might take some time.

He had brought ten people with him to capture Faulke. The office had an android guard, though, the durable kind used in prisons. Koos either had to disable it or get it out of the building.

He'd failed the one time he'd tried to disable those things in the past. He was opting for getting it out of the building.

Ready? he sent to two of his team members.

Yes, they sent back at the same time.

Go! he sent.

They were nowhere near him, but he knew what they were going to do. They were going to start a fight in front of the building that would get progressively more violent. And then they'd start shooting up the area with laser pistols.

Other members of his team would prevent any locals from stopping the fight, and the fight would continue until the guard came down.

Then Koos would sneak in the back way, along with three other members of his team.

They were waiting now. They had already checked the back door—unlocked during daylight hours. They were talking as if they had some kind of business with each other.

At least they weren't shifting from foot to foot like he wanted to do.

Instead, all he could do was stare at that stamp for Ansel Management.

It hadn't been much work to pick up the Mycenae clone and stuff her into one of the crates.

If Deshin hadn't given the no-kill order, then Koos would have stuffed Faulke into one of the crates, dying, but alive, so that he knew what he had done.

Koos would have preferred that to Deshin's plan.

But Koos wasn't in charge. And he had to work his way back into Deshin's good graces.

And he would do that.

Starting now.

19

GUMIELA HAD FORGOTTEN that Ike Jarvis was an officious prick. He ran intelligence operatives who worked inside the Alliance. Generally, those operatives didn't operate in human-run areas. In fact, they shouldn't operate in human-run areas at all.

Earth Alliance Intelligence was supposed to do the bulk of its work *outside* the Alliance.

Gumiela had contacted him on a special link the Earth Alliance had set up for the Armstrong Police Department, to be used only in cases of Earth Alliance troubles or serious Alliance issues.

She figured this counted.

Jarvis appeared in the center of the room, his three-dimensional image fritzing in and out either because of a bad connection or because of the levels of encoding this conversation was going through.

He looked better when he appeared and disappeared. She preferred it when he was slightly out of focus.

"This had better be good, Andy," Jarvis said, and Gumiela felt her shoulders stiffen. No one called her Andy, not even her best friends. Only Jarvis had come up with that nickname, and somehow he seemed to believe it made them closer.

"I need you to pull Cade Faulke," she said.

"I don't pull anyone on your say so." Jarvis fritzed again. His image came back just a little smaller, just a little tighter. So the problem was on his end.

If she were in a better mood, she would smile. Jarvis was short enough without doctoring the image. He had once tried to compensate for his height by buying enhancements that deepened his voice. All they had done was ruin it, leaving him sounding like he had poured salt down his throat.

"You pull him or I arrest him for attempted mass murder," she said, a little surprised at herself.

Jarvis moved and fritzed again. Apparently he had taken a step backwards or something, startled by her vehemence.

"What the hell did he do?" Jarvis asked, not playing games any longer.

"You have Faulke running slow-grow clones in criminal organizations, right?" she asked.

"Andy," he said, returning to that condescending tone he had used earlier, "I can't tell you what I'm doing."

"Fine," she snapped. "I thought we had a courteous relationship, based on mutual interest. I was wrong. Sorry to bother you, Ike—"

"Wait," he said. "What did he do?"

"It doesn't matter," she said. "You get to send Earth Alliance lawyers here to talk about the top-secret crap to judges who might've died because of your guy's carelessness."

And then she signed off.

She couldn't do anything she had just threatened Jarvis with. The food thing hadn't risen to the level where she could charge Faulke, and that was if she could prove that he had put the bodies into the crates himself. He had an android guard, which the Chief of Police had had to approve—those things weren't supposed to operate inside the city—and that guard had probably done all the dirty work. They would just claim malfunction, and Faulke would be off the hook.

Jarvis fritzed back in, fainter now. The image had one meter sideways, which meant he was superimposed over one of her office chairs. The chair cut through him at his knees and waist. Obviously, he had no idea where his image had appeared, and she wasn't about to tell him or move the image.

"Okay, okay," Jarvis said. "I've managed to make this link as secure as I possibly can, given my location. Guarantee that your side is secure."

Gumiela shrugged. "I'm alone in my office, in the Armstrong Police Department. Good enough for you?"

She didn't tell him that she was recording this whole thing. She was tired of being used by this asshole.

"I guess it'll have to be. Yes, Faulke is running the clones that we have embedded with major criminal organizations on the Moon."

"If the clones malfunction—" She chose that word carefully "—what's he supposed to do?"

"Depends on how specific the clone is to the job, and how important it is to the operation," he said. "Generally, Faulke's supposed to ship the clone back. That's why Armstrong PD approved android guards for his office."

"There aren't guards," she said. "There's only one."

Jarvis's image came in a bit stronger. "What?"

"Just one," she said, "and that's not all. I don't think your friend Faulke has sent any clones back."

"I can check," Jarvis said.

"I don't care what you do for your records. According to ours—" and there she was lying again— "he's been killing the clones that don't work out and putting them in composting crates. Those crates go to the Growing Pits, which grow fresh food for the city."

"He *what?*" Jarvis asked.

"And to make matters worse, he's using a hardening poison to kill them, a poison our coroner fears might leach into our food supply. We're checking on that now. Although it doesn't matter. The intent is what matters, and clearly your man Faulke has lost his mind."

Jarvis cursed. "You're not making this up."

It wasn't a question.

"I'm not making this up," she said. "I want him and his little android friend out of here within the hour, or I'm arresting him, and I'm putting him on trial. Public trial."

"Do you realize how many operations you'll ruin?"

"No," she said, "and I don't care. Get him out of my city. It's only a matter of time before your crazy little operative starts killing legal humans, not just cloned ones. And I don't want him doing it here."

Jarvis cursed again. "Can I get your help—"

"No," she said. "I don't want anyone at the police department involved with your little operation. And if you go to the chief, I'll tell her that you have thwarted my attempts to arrest a man who threatens the entire dome. Because, honestly, Ike *baby*, this is a courtesy contact. I don't have to do you any favors at all, especially considering what kind of person, if I can use that word, you installed in my city. Have you got that?"

"Yes, Andrea, I do," he said, looking serious.

Andrea. So he had heard her all those times. And he had ignored her, the bastard. She made note of that too.

"One hour," she said, and signed off.

Then she wiped her hands on her skirt. They were shaking just a little. Screw him, the weaselly little bastard. She'd send someone to that office now, to escort Jarvis's horrid operative out of Armstrong.

She wanted to make sure that asshole left quickly, and didn't double back.

She wanted this problem out of her city, off her Moon, and as far from her notice as possible.

And that, she knew, was the best she could do without upsetting the department's special relationship with the Alliance.

She hoped her best would be good enough.

20

UP THE BACK STAIRS, into the narrow hallway that smelled faintly of dry plastic, Koos led the raid, his best team members behind him. They fanned out in the narrow hallway, the two women first, signaling that the hallway was clear. Koos and Hala, the only other man on this part of the team, skirted past them, and through the open door of Faulke's office.

It was much smaller than Koos expected. Faulke was only three meters from him. Faulke was scrawny, narrow-shouldered, the kind of man easily ignored on the street.

He reached behind his back—probably for a weapon—as Koos and Hala held their laser rifles on him.

"Don't even try," Koos said. "I have no compunction shooting you."

Faulke's eyes glazed for a half second—probably letting his android guard know he was in trouble—then an expression of panic flitted across his face before he managed to control it.

The other members of Koos's team had already disabled the guard.

"Who are you?" Faulke asked.

Koos ignored him, and spoke to his team. "I want him bound. And make sure you disable his links."

One of the women slipped in around Koos, and put light cuffs around Faulke's wrists and pasted a small rectangle of Silent-Seal over his mouth.

You can't get away with this, Faulke sent on public links. *You have no idea who I am—*

And then his links shut off.

Koos grinned. "You're Cade Faulke. You work for Earth Alliance Intelligence. You've been running clones that you embed into businesses. Am I missing anything?"

Faulke's eyes didn't change, but he swallowed hard.

"Let's get him out of here," Koos said.

They encircled him, in case the other tenants on the floor decided to see what all the fuss was about.

But no one opened any doors. The neighborhood was too dicey for that. If anyone had an ounce of civic feeling, they would have gone out front to stop the fight that Koos had staged below.

And no one had.

He took Faulke's arm, surprised at how flabby it was. Hardly any muscles at all.

No wonder the asshole had used poison. He wasn't strong enough to subdue any living creature on his own.

"You're going to love what we have planned for you," Koos said as he dragged Faulke down the stairs. "By the end of it all, you and I will be old friends."

This time Faulke gave him a startled look.

Koos grinned at him, and led him to the waiting car that would take them to the Port.

It would be a long time before anyone heard from Cade Faulke again.

If they ever did.

21

DERICCI HATED DAYS like today. She had lost a case because of stupid laws that had no bearing on what really happened.

A woman had been murdered, and DeRicci couldn't solve the case. It would go to Property, where it would get stuck in a pile of cases that no one cared about, because no one would be able to put a value on this particular clone. No owner would come forward. No one would care.

And if DeRicci hadn't seen this sort of thing a dozen times, she would have tried to solve it herself in her off time. She might still hound Property, just to make sure the case didn't get buried.

Maybe she'd even use Broduer's lies. She might tell Property that whoever planted the clone had tried to poison the city. That might get some dumb Property detective off his butt.

She, on the other hand, was already working on the one good thing to come out of this long day. She was compiling all the documents on every single thing that Rayvon Lake had screwed up in their short tenure as partners.

Even she hadn't realized how much it was.

She would have a long list for Gumiela by the end of the day, and this time, Gumiela would pay attention.

Or DeRicci would threaten to take the clone case to the media. DeRicci had been appalled that human waste could get into the recycling system; she would wager that the population of Armstrong would too.

One threat like that, and Gumiela would have to fire Lake.

It wasn't justice. It wasn't anything resembling justice.

But after a few years in this job, DeRicci had learned only one thing:

Justice didn't exist in the Earth Alliance.

Not for humans, not for clones, not for anyone.

And somehow, she had to live with it.

She just hadn't quite figured out how.

22

DESHIN ARRIVED HOME, exhausted and more than a little unsettled. The house smelled of baby powder and coffee. He hadn't really checked to see how the rest of Gerda's day alone with Paavo had gone.

He felt guilty about that.

He went through the modest living room to the baby's room. He and Gerda didn't flash their wealth around Armstrong, preferring to live quietly. But he had so much security in the home that he was still startled the clone had broken through it.

Gerda was sitting in a rocking chair near the window, Paavo in her arms. She put a finger to her lips, but it did no good.

His five-month-old son twisted, and looked at Deshin with such aware eyes that it humbled him. Deshin knew that this baby was twenty times smarter than he would ever be. It worried him, and it pleased him as well.

Paavo smiled and extended his pudgy arms. Deshin picked him up. The boy was heavier than he had been just a week before. He also needed a diaper change.

Deshin took him to the changing table, and started, knowing just from the look on her face that Gerda was exhausted too.

"Long day?" he asked.

"Good day," she said. "We made the right decision."

"Yes," he said. "We did."

He had decided on the way home not to tell her everything. He would wait until the interrogation of Cade Faulke and the five clones was over. Koos had taken all six of them out of Armstrong in the same ship.

And the interrogations wouldn't even start until Koos got them out of Earth Alliance territory, days from now.

Deshin had no idea what would happen to Faulke or the clones after that. Deshin was leaving that up to Koos. Koos no longer headed security for Deshin Enterprises in Armstrong, but he had served Deshin well today. He would handle some of the company's work outside the Alliance.

Not a perfect day's work, not even the day's work Deshin had expected, but a good one nonetheless. He probably had other leaks to plug in his organization, but at least he knew what they were now.

His baby raised a chubby fist at Deshin as if agreeing that action needed to be taken. Deshin bent over and blew bubbles on Paavo's tummy, something that always made Paavo giggle.

He giggled now, a sound so infectious that Deshin wondered how he had lived without it all his life.

He would do everything he could to protect this baby, everything he could to take care of his family.

"He trusts you," Gerda said with a tiny bit of amazement in her voice.

Most people never trusted Deshin. Gerda did, but Gerda was special.

Deshin blew bubbles on Paavo's tummy again, and Paavo laughed.

His boy did trust him.

He picked up his newly diapered son, and cradled him in his arms. Then he kissed Gerda.

The three of them, forever.

That was what he needed, and that was what he ensured today.

The detective could poke around his business all she wanted, but she would never know the one thing that calmed Deshin down.

Justice had been done.

His family was safe.

And that was all that mattered.

If you liked this novella, you might enjoy
the entire eight-book Anniversary Day Saga,
which is available now in ebook, paperback
and audiobook from your favorite bookseller.

Turn the page for a sample of the first book
in the Saga: *Anniversary Day.*

THE BOMBING
(FOUR YEARS AGO)

1

BARTHOLOMEW NYQUIST PARKED his aircar in one of the hoverlots at the end of the neighborhood. The dome was dark this morning, even though someone should have started the Dome Daylight program. Maybe they had, deciding that Armstrong was in for a "cloudy" day—terminology he never entirely understood, given that the Moon had no clouds and most people who lived here had been born on the Moon and had never seen a cloud in their entire lives.

He grabbed his laser pistol from the passenger seat. He always kept the pistol on the passenger seat when he was traveling, just in case something happened. He tucked the pistol in his shoulder holster, hidden under his already-rumpled suit coat, and got out of the car.

The neighborhood looked even darker than it should have, sprawled below him like something out of those Dickens Christmas plays his ex-wife loved so much. All it needed was some sooty smoke coming out of chimneys above each house to be authentically dreary.

Oh, his mood was bad. And for that, he could probably only blame himself. He should "buck up"—wasn't that what Chief of the First Detective Unit, Andrea Gumiela, had told him yesterday? *Buck up, Bartholomew. Everyone gets divorced. And yours was two years ago. The attitude was understandable last year. This year, it's becoming a problem.*

That after she made him watch the entire complaint vid his now-former partner had filed. Nyquist knew the complaints already, having heard them from previous partners and in his divorce proceeding: surly, impossible to work with, superior. Conversations filled with biting sarcasm—and that was on a good day. On a bad day, he didn't communicate at all.

And on this day, he didn't have to. Still on the force, still a homicide detective, and still without a new partner. He would have partner tryouts all week. The brass wanted to keep Nyquist. He had the best closing rate on the force. The problem was that regulations stated he needed a partner. He stated that he didn't. He worked better alone.

Gumiela knew that, but she followed the rules. Which was why she was his boss instead of the other way around.

Nyquist took the stairs to the sidewalk. He hated these cases in the outer districts of Armstrong. The row houses here rented for less than apartments downtown, but apartments were nicer. A lot of these houses had landlords who only owned one or two properties, and couldn't afford the upkeep. It showed in dingy walls that hadn't been upgraded in decades. Moon dust stains still clung to some of the siding, even though Moon dust had been cleared out of this area since the dome improvements two decades ago.

Not every part of the city was Moon-dust free, particularly Old Armstrong, which had stupid historic regulations that prevented certain kinds of upkeep. But Nyquist knew this neighborhood didn't have that kind of regulation, and so the lack of upkeep was either a financial or a business decision.

Not that he cared about the upkeep of houses as it pertained to regulations. He cared about it as it pertained to the kind of people living inside—people on the edge of hopelessness, people whose economic future wasn't quite bleak but could be with just one disaster, one horrible thing gone wrong.

When he reached the street, he peered around the corner, saw two squads, white-and-blue lights turning, crime scene lasers already up. He should've parked down here, but he'd needed the walk. Besides, on days like this, he didn't want to be part of the squad. He liked being on his own, and parking his car away from the scene let him keep his autonomy.

He knew he would need it.

He sighed. He was supposed to contact Dispatch the moment he arrived in the neighborhood and he'd been putting it off. He knew what they would say. A tryout partner would be waiting for him at the scene. Gumiela had already done this to him once. A tryout partner on scene showed the brass whether or not Nyquist and the newbie worked well together.

It also prevented Nyquist from rejecting the new partner outright, based on clothes, appearance, or general lack of verbal defensive ability.

The question was which of those people loitering outside the crime scene was the one he'd be stuck with all day long.

Couldn't put it off any longer. He sent a ping to Dispatch through his links, hoping they'd only look at his location and not try to contact him.

Instead, a tiny image of this morning's dispatch—a woman with dark hair and matching dark circles under her eyes—appeared in the lower left corner of his vision. He hated that most of all. Couldn't they just use audio like everyone else on the Force?

"Detective Nyquist." It looked like she was speaking aloud as well as sending through the links. For the record? Probably. No one wanted to get in trouble because *he* got in trouble. "You'll be meeting your new partner at the scene. Her name is Ursula Palmette—"

Newly Minted Detective. I got it, he sent, deliberately not speaking out loud for any record.

"No, detective, not that newly minted at all. She has worked as a detective for five months."

What happened to her training partner? he sent. He stopped only a few meters from the house that seemed to be the center of attention. He didn't want to go any further while having this conversation.

"Early retirement," the dispatch said.

For some bad conduct? Nyquist sent.

"No, sir. Family troubles. His wife is dying and he didn't want to spend the last year of her life working."

That surprised him. He felt color touch his cheeks, something that didn't happen to him often. He was glad it happened before he met Palmette. He didn't want to step in it at the very beginning of their relationship.

All right, he sent, not acknowledging his discomfort or the slight reprimand the dispatch had given him. *Anything else I need to know?*

"Just that the officers on site say that they're ready for you, sir."

He was beginning to seriously dislike this dispatch. Who was she to subtly reprimand him like that?

Instead of challenging her, he just severed the link and walked the remaining few meters to the crime scene. Police line lasers gave the fake grass a reddish tint. An ambulance was parked sideways behind one of the squad cars, lights off.

He found that a curious detail. Either the ambulance wasn't needed and it could go off elsewhere, or it was needed and it had to stay, in which case its warning lights would be on low.

Two officers stood in front of the crime scene lasers. A tiny woman with a cap of brown hair leaned against one of the squads, holding a steaming cup of something—probably coffee—in her right hand.

As Nyquist approached, she stood.

"Detective Nyquist," she said. "I'm—"

"Ursula Palmette," he said, resisting the urge to add "newly minted detective." "I suppose you have documentation for me?"

She extended her hand. He hated chip-to-chip information transfer, but it was department policy these days. He grabbed her hand in a relatively loose grip, and felt the chip in the center of his palm warm, which was a signal that the information exchange was not only complete but accepted.

In the past, he'd go through a speech—*I'm the lead on this case. You shouldn't question my authority. I'll do all the talking*—but she already had had a training officer and she should know this crap. Besides, he'd been told by his previous two partners that his little opening speech was off-putting. He decided not to put Detective Ursula Palmette off. He simply did not have the energy for it.

"What do we know?" he asked.

"Well, sir," she said, then paused. "It is sir, right? Or do you prefer Detective? Or Bartholomew?"

"I prefer to know why the hell I'm here." He hated all the protocol with names. He certainly wasn't going to let her call him Bartholomew, which seemed to be what she was angling for. He didn't like casual relationships between partners. He preferred formality. She'd figure it out.

She nodded. She couldn't have been more than thirty, with that fresh-faced, straight-out-of-the-academy look. He preferred his partners to have worked their way to the detective squad, not get fast-tracked through so-called police education.

He didn't say that, which he would have had he met her in the precinct. Instead, he watched her peel the lid off her drink, which made it steam all the more, sending a smell of cinnamon and milk into the air, turning his stomach. She took a sip before saying anything else, as if the drink fortified her somehow.

"Um," she said, pressing the lid back on the cup. "We have a body—"

He resisted the urge to roll his eyes. Of course they had a body. They were *homicide* detectives. Someone had to die for the street cops to call him in.

"—in the front room of the house. The woman inside called it in. The responding officers say something is a little off in the entire thing."

"A little off?" Nyquist said.

Palmette shrugged. "Their words. You can talk to them. I was instructed not to do any investigating until you arrived."

Because he had the high closure rate, and one of his complaints about partners was that they made his job harder, not easier. They asked the wrong questions, contaminated crime scenes all by their little lonesome, and compromised witnesses.

"And yet you know about the body, and the scene being a little off," he said.

"Because Officer Saxe—," and she nodded at a young cop with curly red hair and copper skin standing near one of the squads, "—told me the minute I arrived. I told him we had to wait for you, and so he stopped. You want to talk to him now, sir?"

So she was going to stick with "sir." Fine.

"No," Nyquist said. "I want to see the interior. Got a suit?"

By that, he meant protective covering for her skin and clothes. Most rookie detectives had to make do with the full-body suits that the cops gave to civilians at crime scenes, but she tapped her arm.

"Already on, sir," she said.

That was when he noticed that her clothes were just a bit shiny. He took one of his protective suits out of the pocket of his coat. The suit was the size of his thumbnail, until he attached it to the button on his sleeve and tapped it.

Then the damn thing enveloped him. He hated that moment—it felt like walking into a gigantic spider web, which he had done once as a kid on vacation with his parents on Earth—and then the feeling went away.

"Okay," he said as he blocked the crime scene laser with his palm. Another chip on his palm made sure that none of the warning sirens went off. He stepped onto the fake grass and waited for Palmette to join him. "Let's see what we've got."

Be the first to know!

Just sign up for the Kristine Kathryn Rusch newsletter, and keep up with the latest news, releases and so much more—even the occasional giveaway.

To sign up, go to kristinekathrynrusch.com.

But wait! There's more. Sign up for the WMG Publishing newsletter, too, and get the latest news and releases from all of the WMG authors and lines, including Kristine Grayson, Kris Nelscott, Dean Wesley Smith, *Fiction River: An Original Anthology Magazine*, *Smith's Monthly*, and so much more.

Just go to wmgpublishing.com and click on Newsletter.

ABOUT THE AUTHOR

New York Times bestselling author Kristine Kathryn Rusch writes in almost every genre. Generally, she uses her real name (Rusch) for most of her writing. Under that name, she publishes bestselling science fiction and fantasy, award-winning mysteries, acclaimed mainstream fiction, controversial nonfiction, and the occasional romance. Her novels have made bestseller lists around the world and her short fiction has appeared in eighteen best of the year collections. She has won more than twenty-five awards for her fiction, including the Hugo, *Le Prix Imaginales,* the *Asimov's* Readers Choice award, and the *Ellery Queen Mystery Magazine* Readers Choice Award.

To keep up with everything she does, go to kriswrites.com. To track her many pen names and series, see their individual websites (krisnelscott.com, kristinegrayson.com, krisdelake.com, retrievalartist. com, divingintothewreck.com, fictionriver.com). She lives and occasionally sleeps in Oregon.